As Bolan sighted along the 93-R, he saw someone lining up on him

Downrange a shotgun boomed and Bolan dived toward the hedge, his combat senses propelling him to action before he could assimilate the situation.

He lifted his head and parted the shrubbery, trying to get a better look at his armed adversary. He saw a tall blond man grasping a battle shotgun. There were two other guys with him.

Bolan blinked, shut his eyes, then opened them again. No. it couldn't be—

The Executioner suddenly knew who was firing at him.

Able Team!

MACK BOLAN

The Executioner

DON PENDLETON's EXECUTIONER
MACK BOLAN
Death Games

A GOLD EAGLE BOOK FROM
W🌐RLDWIDE

TORONTO · NEW YORK · LONDON · PARIS
AMSTERDAM · STOCKHOLM · HAMBURG
ATHENS · MILAN · TOKYO · SYDNEY

First edition June 1985

ISBN 0-373-61078-5

Special thanks and acknowledgment to
Tom Arnett for his contributions to this work.

Printed in Canada

Morality is the herd-instinct in the individual.
                              —*Nietzsche*

This is war, and there is no such thing as
morality in warfare.
                              —*Mack Bolan*

To the U.S. servicemen and their spouses,
and other non-Americans,
who were injured in the Athens, Greece, bomb blast.
Portent of a new wave of terrorism?

1

Mack Bolan crouched in the shadow of a thick hedge. He remained as motionless as the statue, five feet away from him, that kept its nocturnal vigil on Vienna's Stadtpark.

The Executioner's eyes were trained on the two men who stood at the base of the Johann Strauss monument. Bolan knew the duo, or their reputation, at any rate.

The taller of the pair was General Leopold Abovian, top KGB cannibal and mind-control specialist. His counterpart was Cuban, Colonel Fernandez Maceo.

The nightstalker had followed the two men to this nighttime rendezvous in the Austrian city, and the Executioner was laying bets that something dirty was going down.

Suddenly, movement to his right alerted Bolan, and in the harsh spill of light from the nearby lamp standards he saw two women approaching from the direction of the Intercontinental Hotel. They appeared to be tourists, but a warning tingle settled at the base of Bolan's neck as he watched them veer off the concrete path to intercept three new arrivals.

A blond woman, walking with the bearing of someone who has had military training, was flanked by two male escorts. Both men had their hands stuck in jacket pockets, and Bolan had no trouble placing them as some kind of security for their blond charge.

The big warrior remained concealed in the shadow of the hedge. Beyond the lights' glare, still more movement caught his attention. He could barely discern three other figures scurrying to the perimeter of whatever action was about to take place.

Now what the hell. . . ?

Bolan's battle instincts flared. Whatever was going down here tonight had more wild cards than a Vegas casino.

Abovian's calm voice broke into Bolan's thoughts as the Russian spoke to his companion.

"Your subject should be turning herself over to the Americans soon. Do your men know what to do?"

Maceo snorted and when he replied his tone told Bolan that he considered the general's words to be an affront.

"But of course, Comrade General."

"And are you satisfied with the preparation of your subject?"

The Cuban colonel's heavily accented reply contrasted sharply to the Russian's crisp English. "*Sí.* She thinks she acts of her own will. Only the face of her target will trigger her to kill. I am sad to lose her. She was an efficient assistant."

"Then I suggest we retreat." The two men began to walk away.

Bolan decided he could pick up the trail of the two cannibals later.

The blonde and her guards were now within a few feet of Bolan's position when one of the men said something to her in Spanish. It sounded like a trivial remark, and her answer had nothing to do with the question.

"I do not wish to go with you. Leave me alone."

The night warrior frowned when pistols materialized in the fists of the other two women the moment the blonde spoke. As if on cue, her guards broke for an exit out of the park. Too smooth. The whole exercise was phony.

Suddenly Bolan realized that he was witnessing the transfer of a defector who was programmed to kill.

Although it had started out as a soft probe, the Executioner was rigged for battle. Years of fighting in the hellgrounds had shown Bolan that innocent probes could turn hard in a heartbeat. And the soldier was taking no chances this night. Combat senses told him that all hell was about to erupt.

The Beretta 93-R nestled in a shoulder speed rig, and Big Thunder, the awesome .44 AutoMag, rode the warrior's hip. Bolan pulled the 93-R from its holster as he began to rise from his crouch. The sleek weapon nosed out ahead of him, panning the darkness.

He couldn't afford to let that human time bomb

fulfill its deadly destiny. And there was no way of knowing how soon she'd see her target. Grim experience told the big soldier that if she'd been Maceo's assistant, she wouldn't remain in American hands long enough to talk. She'd have a death sentence riding on her head if she failed in her mission.

The Executioner recognized the suck play. As long as Abovian and the Cuban savage were involved, someone in the West was marked for death. Bolan knew he had to take out the guinea pig before she reached her target.

Bolan sighted down the barrel of the sleek Beretta. It would be a difficult shot in the poor light. He had to hit his moving mark without wounding one of the women with her. As he drew his bead his peripheral vision told him that one of the three men who had been covering the women from a distance had swung up a weapon. A shotgun boomed and the Executioner dived for the base of the hedge, his combat senses propelling him to action before he could realistically assimilate the situation.

Bolan bellied a few feet away from the spot where he landed. He spent some precious moments assessing the odds. One against three and whoever else might decide to show up. No matter. One thing was certain. Those guys were there to protect the blonde and her two female companions.

Bolan lifted his head and peered into the distance. The three women were still calmly retreating as if they were taking a Sunday stroll in the park. The soldier parted the shrubbery to get a better look at his armed adversaries.

He saw a tall man with blond hair grasping a battle shotgun. There were two other guys with him. Bolan blinked, shut his eyes, then opened them again. No, it couldn't be—

The Executioner suddenly knew who was firing at him.

Able Team!

The big nightfighter stood up and holstered his Beretta. He moved forward and called out softly, "Carl."

The weapon roared again and a shower of steel balls peppered the spot in the hedge that Bolan occupied only seconds before. Bolan hit the grass, listening to the pellets whistle through the hedge. Then the echo of the firestorm subsided, leaving a ringing silence in its wake.

The twin tubes of Lyons's weapon were sweeping the length of the hedge and Bolan sprinted for the plinth of the statue a heartbeat before the shotgun opened up again.

The Executioner scowled as he leaned against the concrete base of the monument.

Since he had severed official links with Stony Man Farm, Bolan had retained only intermittent contact with the men of Able Team and Phoenix Force. Perhaps the "Terminate on Sight" order on him had been reinstated. But Hal Brognola would have warned him, sure.

The Executioner refused to acknowledge this.

There must be a good reason why Able Team was trying to kill him. He had recognized the trio, even in the half light. Surely they in turn would know it was he. Still. . .

The soldier had always depended on the slim advantage of surprise, right. Now it was working against him. He was certain Carl Lyons had not expected to see anyone even remotely resembling Mack Bolan in this godforsaken place.

There were a couple of confrontations many lives ago, when Lyons, as a member of the LAPD, had the drop on Bolan, and each time he had let Bolan walk away. Years later, as the head of the Phoenix program, Bolan and Lyons had fought side by side in the hellgrounds. And this was why the soldier refused to believe Lyons was trying to kill him.

But Mack Bolan had not survived this long in his everlasting war by taking unnecessary risks or playing useless guessing games.

His hand hesitated for only a fraction of a second near his right hip before he grasped the Auto-Mag's butt firmly, tugged it free and thumbed the hammer back. The click was deafening in the night silence. . . .

"COME IN, JACK. Do you read me, Skyboy?" Gadgets Schwarz said, pressing a miniature transceiver to his lips.

Pol Blancanales hovered over Schwarz's crouched form, listening as he tried to raise the Stony Man pilot.

Carl Lyons kept covering his partners when he heard a loud click and pivoted to see a big apparition in black clutching a handgun and coming toward them. The figure was still too far away to discern any features, and Lyons swung up the shotgun.

The man appeared to pose no threat, and somehow his movement seemed familiar to Lyons, but any attempt at recognition eluded him. He lifted the shotgun to his shoulder, his finger caressing the trigger.

The newcomer was closing in when Blancanales yelled, "Carl, don't shoot!" and slammed a fist down on the barrel of Lyons's weapon.

"Thanks, Pol. How quickly they forget," Bolan said, holstering the .44.

The deep voice was unmistakable.

"Mack!" Lyons said sheepishly. "You're the last person we expected to find here. Besides, I saw you lining up on Pitt. Our job's to keep her alive."

The two women and their blond companion had stopped two hundred yards away. They were waiting for Able Team to catch up. They kept glancing around nervously.

Lyons checked Wendy Pitt's location, decided that she was safe for the moment and approached Bolan. Police sirens were wailing. Gadgets continued to try to raise Jack Grimaldi, the Stony Man flying ace. He got no response.

Bolan stopped. "What happened to Jack?"

"The last time he made contact he said something about MiGs and a crash landing. We haven't been able to raise him since.''

''Which approach was he planning to use?''

''He planned to make a wide sweep and come in from the northeast,'' Lyons answered.

''That would take him close to the Czechoslovakia border. You'd better get out of here and commandeer something at the airport. I'll try to find out what happened to Jack. By the way, whoever that blonde is, she's been programmed to kill someone.''

''What? But she's valuable. Her father's Senator Andrew Pitt, and she's Castro's expert in the logistics and support of his terrorists. The two women with her are CIA operatives. If we lose her, the President will pull Stony Man apart.''

''Maybe her father is the target.''

Bolan knew the numbers were running out for Able Team. If they were caught, the United States would deny any knowledge of the affair. He sighed as he realized he had made the right decision when he quit Stony Man Farm.

The Executioner left them to it and jogged through the shadows to his Moskvitch, which he had parked near the hotel.

There was no time to change from his black skinsuit, but he had been prepared for that. Bolan quickly shrugged on a white shirt, tie and a dinner jacket.

As soon as the jacket was buttoned over his combat gear, he jumped into the car and pulled out into traffic. Bolan traveled less than two hundred yards before a policeman waved him to the curb. The Executioner stopped the car and wound down the driver's window.

The officer spoke in rapid German, which Bolan was unable to follow. He raised his palm and shook his head to indicate he spoke no German. In any case, he didn't dare spend much time talking to the police. Not if he wanted to find out what happened to Grimaldi.

Bolan lapsed into Russian and thrust the false Russian identity papers, which had been provided by friendly Afghans and identified Bolan as a Russian trade official.

The policeman shook his head.

With a Russian accent, Bolan said in English, "Here are my papers." He smiled, looking as if he was trying to be helpful.

"Ah, the English I can speak," the cop said, beaming. He appeared happy to establish communication.

The officer looked at the documents, then at Bolan. "Mr. Dostenko, where have you been so late in the evening?"

"At the American Embassy, listening to them tell me how peaceful they are."

"You were there until this late?" The policeman was looking at him speculatively.

Bolan shrugged. "Well...there is an American translator there. Very beautiful. We stayed and talked for a long time."

The officer handed back the papers. "Did you hear any shooting as you drove past the park?"

"No. What is happening?"

"We do not know, yet. You are free to go."

His identity established, Bolan decided to push his luck. Finding Jack Grimaldi would be a huge problem; Bolan could not afford to pass up any opportunity for information.

"The truth is, officer, I was called away from a pleasant interlude. It seems that some of our planes violated Austrian airspace. Have you heard anything about it?"

The policeman studied Bolan's face before answering. Bolan knew he was remembering the face of a Russian spy to report to his superiors.

After a brief silence, the officer said, "Yes, two of your planes and a helicopter forced down an American helicopter near Gaserndorf. I understand the Russian helicopter landed and took away the pilot of the American aircraft."

"How unfortunate."

The policeman's manner became cold and formal. "Unfortunate, yes. But I suppose we should be thankful that it was not a passenger liner." He waved for Bolan to move on.

Bolan began to circle toward the Intercontinental Hotel. He had to find Abovian, fast.

JACK GRIMALDI had been expecting a piece of cake. It had seemed like such a simple job: land the Sikorsky S-55 in the park, pick up Able Team, two CIA operatives and a defector, fly them to Trieste where a military jet waited to transport everybody back to the States.

Now Grimaldi was sure the MiGs had been waiting for him. He had no idea how they knew he'd be there, but as he began the long runback into Vienna, over the airport to drop into the park, the MiGs came screaming down at him from high altitude.

Jack had slapped the chopper into autorotation and the huge Sikorsky dropped like a stone. Right into the path of an MI-24 Hind assault helicopter.

The Russians had waited until he was almost stationary and then their cannon had taken off the main rotor. Only the size of the Sikorsky and the well-built pilot's seat prevented Jack from disintegrating along with the chopper.

The Hind touched down almost at the same time beside the wrecked helicopter. Jack was still dazed and bleeding from the nose when two soldiers dragged him free of the wreckage. By the time he had collected his wits sufficiently to resist, he found himself handcuffed and hoisted aboard the Russian chopper. And when the cobwebs had cleared from Jack's brain, he was already being flown over Czechoslovakian territory.

Jack gave a sigh for an interesting life. No one was going to be able to find him behind the iron curtain.

GENERAL ABOVIAN CRADLED THE TELEPHONE receiver and raised his glass of vodka in a toast to good fortune.

"It was as we had calculated," he told Maceo. "We have the special pilot these people use. Now, if Wendy Pitt fails in her mission, then we shall use the pilot as bait to get our man. He has been inside Russia before and our files tell us that nothing will stop him from attempting to rescue his pilot. One way or the other we shall capture him.''

Maceo felt slightly annoyed as he leaned back in the ornate chair in the general's hotel suite, sipping his rum. It was all very well for Abovian to gloat; he didn't have to go into the United States to supervise the next phase of the plan. Perhaps a small dig was in order.

"What about the CIA *puercos* who go with her? Do they get an easy ride?''

"No. Those fighters are good. But if none of them gets killed, the Americans will begin to suspect that the transfer was too easy. We shall eliminate most of them before they leave Europe. That way the CIA will be convinced we did our best to stop her.''

Maceo was perplexed. "Then should we not be doing something?''

Abovian grinned like a hungry wolf. "It's all arranged. Very few of those Americans will see their native soil again. There are snipers covering all points of departure.''

2

Able Team caught up with the two CIA agents and Wendy Pitt before they reached the southwest corner of Stadtpark. Police cars had already blocked the intersection of Johannesgasse and Parkring roads.

Blancanales looked at Wendy Pitt's face, and Bolan's words came back to him: "She's been programmed to kill someone." Pol knew that he should not let the woman's innocent features deceive him. As long as Able Team fulfilled its mission—protecting and delivering Wendy Pitt— then perhaps he need not concern himself about who or what she was.

"Where are we going?" she asked, disrupting Pol's train of thought.

Politician glanced up at the Kursalon. "The terrace is closed, but the café inside seems to be open. I think we should hole up until the heat is off. The place is crawling with cops."

She looked at him quizzically, unable to understand his English.

Lyons caught on immediately. "A great idea. Let's move it!"

Gadgets opened the gym bag he was carrying.

Each member of the team quickly tossed in his large weapon and ammunition. Handguns were already concealed in breakaway rigs under their jackets. Gadgets quickly zipped the bag shut and slung it over his shoulder.

Pol offered Wendy his arm. Looking still more puzzled, she placed a small hand in his, rather than merely holding on to his arm. Carl Lyons grabbed the two CIA women by the elbows and growled, "On the double."

Able Team and the three women descended on the restaurant in the park.

The maitre d' who was lounging at the entrance of the empty hostelry was surprised to have a party of six appear so late. He hurried forward, his hands raised in protest.

Diplomacy was Pol's department. He reached into his trouser pocket and produced a wad of 1,000-schilling notes. He seized an outstretched hand and counted four notes into it.

The man smiled and then said in English, "What can we do for you?"

"Food. I'll double that tip if we have our appetizers within five minutes."

The maitre d' turned and barked orders to two waiters.

Three minutes later, when two police officers came into the restaurant, there was only one group left. They were sipping wine and eating paté on flat bread. A waiter was putting a platter of grilled mushrooms on the table. The diners were talking with the slight boisterousness of tourists who have spent too long sampling the strong Voslauer wines.

"Anyone run through here recently?" a policeman asked.

The maitre d' pointed to Able Team and the women. The cop smiled and shook his head.

"Not at all what we're looking for. Americans?"

"I suspect so."

"Crass, but so full of life. I suppose I should speak to them."

The officer could manage English fairly well. "Good evening, *mein Herren*," he said, approaching the table.

The big blond man turned those ice-blue eyes toward him and the officer was not at all sure that this would be a simple conversation.

"I am told that you arrived at this restaurant not too long ago."

The man with the white hair and dark, arched eyebrows took a sip of wine before answering. "We've barely sat down."

The policeman looked at the wineglasses and the half-consumed food. The American was using a figure of speech. "Did you hear the sounds of shooting coming from the park?"

The group exchanged blank looks and shook their heads.

The policeman thanked them, wished them a pleasant stay in Vienna, and left.

One of the CIA agents, a robust woman in her early forties, said, "Shouldn't we be getting out of here?"

"The police are out there. Let's give them time to do their business and leave. Our transportation is gone. We have some time to kill before taking the alternative way out of the country," Gadgets explained.

"We have an alternate plan?"

Blancanales nodded.

The two CIA women looked nonplussed. Wendy Pitt turned to the Able Team leader. "The pilot who is missing, he is a friend, no?"

"Un compañero estimado," Pol assured her.

Wendy nodded in silent sympathy. Pol was glad she did not express false sentiments of her own. He decided he would have to explain to the others what was happening.

"We were to be picked up by helicopter and flown to Venice, where a U.S. military jet is waiting to take us to the States. By the time we finish this meal, it'll be getting light. We'll walk to the West Station and grab the early train for Udine. There, we can change trains and be in Venice before supper. Any questions?"

"Why the train?" one woman asked. "Won't we be committing ourselves to one vehicle for too long?"

Blancanales looked at the CIA agent. "The problem isn't with the trip. It's getting Miss Pitt out of Vienna alive. The railway station is difficult to cover and probably won't be well watched. Once on the train, we should be okay."

"Please call me Wendy," Pitt told Blancanales. "What do I call you?"

The CIA types were studiously deaf to the question. When it became apparent they had no intention of introducing themselves, Pol answered the blonde.

Although he was as unwilling as the CIA to give even a cover name to someone who had been senior in the Cuban secret police, Pol decided that some risk was necessary, because they would need Pitt's full confidence before the trip was over.

"Call me Pol. This is Gadgets and our blond friend is Ironman."

She smiled at him. "It is understandable that you would not wish your names thrown around in a foreign country. Meeting you makes me glad." She stuck out her hand.

Fifteen minutes later they left the café and trekked through the park in the late dawn. Lyons stopped them when they were still two blocks from the railway station.

"Pol, you're the one who knows the language. Six tickets to Venice and don't forget to check the transfer point at Udine." Then he turned to the two Company agents. "Now's the time to earn your keep. You've got half an hour to patrol the station area and find out if anyone is watching for Miss Pitt. I want to know what we're up against before we go into that station."

While the rest hustled about their assigned tasks, Lyons took Wendy Pitt by the elbow and steered her toward some narrower and dingier streets. Gadgets followed, carrying the bag containing the heavy weapons. Soon they were in an alley where four-story tenements stood side by side for the entire block.

Lyons's eyes darted from left to right, scrutinizing each occupant who emerged from the buildings.

Fifteen minutes later Lyons intercepted a small man descending the steps of a stone house. He was wearing a greasy cloth cap, tweed jacket and a pair of baggy work pants.

Lyons stopped him and pointed to his hat, jacket and pants, then produced two 500-schilling notes. The man seized the money and nodded, understanding at once what the stranger wanted. They followed him back into the house, which was divided into small apartments.

Wendy Pitt quickly changed her clothes, then stuffed her long blond hair under the cloth cap. Soon they were back on the street and hurrying toward Vienna's new West Station.

They found the others waiting impatiently at the spot where the group had split up.

"Only ten minutes to train time," Pol reported.

"We found nothing suspicious. God knows who'd be looking for her," one of the women reported.

The group surrounded Wendy Pitt to make it look as if well-wishers were seeing someone off at the station.

The most important of Vienna's four railway stations had been bombed during World War II. It was replaced by West Station, a modern building of stone, concrete and glass. Above the main-floor entrances and shops a concrete marquee extended out over the unloading zone and the sidewalk, sheltering the area from rain and sun. Two workmen on top of a scaffold were painstakingly using drills and sledges to mount bolts for new signs over each entrance.

As Able Team and their companions hastened into the station, one of the workmen pointed, then both dived for their toolboxes. They produced Steyr 69 SMGs, the Austrian improvement on the Uzi.

Lyons had been carrying his Colt Python under his jacket. Before the "workers" could bring around their submachine guns, the Python roared and the top of one gunman's head exploded into a fountain of crimson. The other gunman got off a short wild burst before two more 158-grain hollowpoints opened up his head like a melon.

The badly aimed bullets caught the CIA operative who was farthest back in the group. Two slugs ripped open her throat and she was thrown onto her back, blood spurting from her neck. Lyons's gun had already disappeared into its breakaway clip, and when the other women hesitated at the sight of their fallen companion, he shoved them violently.

"Move, damn it."

The group kept running toward the station entrance. Blancanales immediately positioned himself behind Wendy Pitt, sheltering her body with his own.

The crack of a high-powered rifle echoed in the

vaulted confines of the station. The bullet barely missed Wendy Pitt. Lyons did not pause to look back. He figured the sniper was working from too far back for handguns to reply.

People were fleeing, stampeding away from the fallen bodies. Able Team and the two remaining women were not conspicuous among the people fighting to reach safety.

The modern electric train was waiting and almost ready to pull out when the group arrived. They stepped into a long open coach with two rows of seats on one side and single seats on another. Passengers watched curiously as the foreigners pleaded until they were allowed to sit together.

Blancanales sat near the window with Wendy on the aisle beside him, across from Lyons. The Company agent sat in front of Lyons. She took her seat in stunned silence, looking distraught. Gadgets chose a seat some distance back where he would have time to move if someone approached the group.

"You just left her lying there in the street like a dog," the CIA agent muttered.

"You think we should have stood around until the sniper got the rest of us?" Lyons grunted.

"But the local police won't know who she is," the woman protested in a whisper.

"I imagine that will save your organization some more embarrassment." Lyons closed the subject.

"It is terrible what happened to that woman," Wendy Pitt whispered to Blancanales.

Pol finished checking out faces in the car as the train pulled out of the station. Only when he was satisfied that he would remember the passengers, did he begin to speak.

"It's one of the risks we take. It's part of the job."

"Will there be more trouble when we arrive?"

"We'll just have to wait and see."

3

Bolan found a spot on a quiet side street and parked the Moskvitch. He drew on a pair of dark blue trousers to match his dinner jacket and a pair of black crepe-soled leather shoes. When he was through, he could have easily passed for a guest of the hotel.

For this probe the soldier had to keep his armament down to a minimum. The silenced 93-R rode in its breakaway clip under his left armpit. Two small defensive grenades scarcely made a bulge in one jacket pocket. A flat Maringer knife lay concealed in a sheath, snug against his forearm.

After a moment's thought he added a pair of tough leather gloves to the other jacket pocket.

Bolan locked the car, then strode boldly into the hotel through the employee entrance. It took him only ten minutes to find the office of the hotel doctor. He made short work of the lock and seconds later he was back in the corridor with a stethoscope stuck into his waistband.

Bolan had already noted the location of Abovian's room, one floor up from the flat roof and to one side, away from the floodlights.

The nighthitter calmly made his way to the roof

and across it, but he took care to walk near the edge, behind the lights. His crepe-soled shoes made no sound on the cement.

When Bolan was directly under Abovian's window, he looked up and to his dismay, realized there was a two-foot gap above him to the cement ledge that ran under the window. He crouched to a squatting position, then unleashed his six-foot frame, arms extended above his head until his fingers gripped the ledge.

Pulling himself onto such a narrow ledge was laborious work. There was no room for error in grip or balance. Bolan slowly dragged himself up, every muscle in his arms screaming protest against his two-hundred-odd pounds.

Finally his torso cleared the ledge after agonizing seconds, and the Executioner slowly straightened his arms until he was able to swing one leg over the parapet. He got his entire body on the concrete lip, then spent a few precious moments gathering his breath, only too aware that the numbers were falling and dawn would soon be upon him.

Bolan stood up and slowly inched sideways on the narrow ledge until he was close to the window. He kept a careful check on his balance, and placed the stethoscope to his ears and the receiver to the windowpane. The voices inside the room were distorted, but he managed to make out the words.

Abovian was saying, "Very few of those Americans will see their native soil again. There are snipers covering all points of departure."

"Then everything is arranged. We can relax," Maceo's high voice said.

"We have no time for relaxation." Abovian's voice carried steel and authority, even through the window glass and stethoscope. "I have a pilot to interrogate. I expect that he has knowledge of every important success the United States has had against us these past five years. You have the entire operation against the Americans. How many men do you have inside their borders?"

"There are 150 trained commandos waiting for me."

The number seemed to startle Abovian as much as it did Mack Bolan. "I am impressed, Colonel. How did you manage that? I thought that you could only trickle in a few whenever the right-wing pigs thought they were smuggling in some of their own."

"The second Bay of Pigs, my General."

"I do not take your meaning."

"I did not study under you for five years and not learn some tricks," said the high-pitched, self-satisfied voice. "It was slow and hard work to smuggle in 150 men I could trust. The reactionaries and the CIA both believe I am training a force to invade my own Cuba."

Abovian laughed. It was not a pleasant laugh, but nevertheless a triumphant one. "A toast to you, Fernandez. Indeed, a clever stroke."

Maceo's laugh sounded more like a girl's giggle. "The CIA were so busy keeping this a secret from their own government that they were most inefficient in checking everything."

"And now, how will you get back to the United States?"

Maceo giggled again. "There is someone with a boat. A gentleman who hates our Fidel very much. He believes I will lead the army that defeats Castro." The giggle came again.

Bolan had heard enough. He removed the stethoscope from the pane. He knew he had to make a decision quickly and that it could lead to disaster. Should he try to warn Able Team? Should he follow Maceo and eliminate him before he could reach the United States and set loose 150 trained terrorists? Or should he follow Abovian back behind the iron curtain and try to rescue Grimaldi?

The jungle fighter jumped off the ledge and landed on all fours, cat-quiet. Still, he turned and looked up at the window to make sure the pair above had not heard him. A bullet in the back could end it all here, the Executioner knew. And too many lives were riding on the line for the soldier to meet his fate on this Austrian rooftop.

Once off the roof, Bolan calmly handed the stethoscope in at the desk, claiming to have found it in the hall. Next, he had to find Abovian's car.

Bolan knew he had to act on faith. A warrior had to have faith in his compatriots or else he rendered himself useless, unable to trust anyone to do anything.

Able Team was walking into a trap. They'd been suckered before and it had been other heads that rolled. Bolan would trust them to handle whatever came up. The same reasoning applied on a larger scale to an enemy force within the boundaries of the United States. Lives might be lost and they might not, but he had to trust the soldiers on the same side to be competent.

No one else was going to help Jack Grimaldi. Able Team was trusting him to do what was necessary. The Executioner would not betray that trust as long as he had life left in him.

The Mercedes that Bolan had followed out of Russia carrying Abovian and Maceo sat in a remote corner of the parking area. Bolan did a careful recon. When he determined that the car wasn't watched, he jogged to his Moskvitch and parked it next to the sleek sedan owned by the general of the People's Army. Bolan unlatched the trunk of the Moskvitch and waited.

Twenty minutes later, the general's chauffeur showed up. The man was still half-asleep, rubbing his eyes and muttering under his breath. The grumbling stopped abruptly when cold steel touched the back of his neck.

"Against the car," Bolan growled in Russian. The icy voice left no room for argument.

The driver did as he was told, then Bolan leathered his 93-R and expertly frisked the man. The only weapon Bolan found was a Yugoslavian Zastava Model 70 with a spare clip. He confiscated it and the car keys.

Bolan stepped back and checked the gun, chambering a round. Then pointing the Zastava at the aide, Bolan told him, "Unload the trunk of the Moskvitch into the trunk of this one."

The Russian hesitated.

"What's your name?" Bolan snapped.

"Nicolai." His voice was sullen.

"I don't have any particular reason to kill you. But I will if I have to."

Nicolai quickly transferred Bolan's case to the trunk of the Mercedes.

"Now, let's not keep the general waiting," Bolan said. He climbed into the back seat as Nicolai slid behind the wheel.

Nicolai drove the Mercedes carefully to the Johannesgasse entrance of the Intercontinental. Abovian was waiting impatiently at the curb.

"Remember," Bolan reminded the aide, "I'll have your gun on the general. Be very careful, or the general will be shot and your gun will be found."

Nicolai left the wheel to store the general's overnight bag in the trunk. The general was halfway into the car when he spotted Bolan with the gun in his hand. Abovian paused for only a second before continuing to slide into the back seat.

The general made himself comfortable before saying, "Colonel Phoenix, I gather."

"You must be mistaken."

The Russian officer shrugged. "Ah, yes. We heard the rumors. But I think that is precisely what they are, rumors. Who are you, then?"

Nicolai slid behind the wheel, carefully keeping his hands in sight.

Abovian turned to the Executioner.

"Where are we going, Mr. . . . ?"

"Igor Dostenko. We are going wherever it was you intended to go. I'm just along for the ride."

"We travel to the Czechoslovakian city you Americans call Kosice. I scarcely expect that is where you wish to go."

"Kosice will do," the Executioner growled.

Abovian nodded for his driver to proceed. Nicolai drove with caution, and Bolan knew that the man was very aware that it was his gun pointed at the general in the back seat.

Through the rooftop window, Bolan had heard Abovian describe Grimaldi as "his pilot." Now the big warrior was certain that the defection of Wendy Pitt and the kidnapping of Grimaldi had been part of an elaborate plot to trap him. His suspicions were confirmed when Abovian called him Colonel Phoenix. Bolan's best guess was that the Russians had heard rumors of his split with Washington but did not believe them.

Bolan's attention was on the rear window, to see if they were being followed. He could detect no car behind them. He heard Abovian chuckling.

"Nervous, my friend? You should be. It's about four hundred kilometers to Kosice. Surely you must realize that it is you who will be my prisoner before the end of this trip."

4

Jack Grimaldi thought he had been through it all. In Nam and again in the firezones with Mack Bolan and the Stony Man teams. Now here he was, blown out of the sky like a skeet and captured. And to top it off, Able Team had no idea of his whereabouts since radio contact was broken. The ace pilot struggled against his bonds in the wooden chair. No use, he figured, when a voice broke into his thoughts.

"You are in Kosice, American. You were forced to land when your helicopter infringed on the territory of the Czechoslovak Socialist Republic."

Jack Grimaldi turned to examine the speaker. The man wore a Russian army uniform, and the insignia indicated he held the rank of major. But Jack was unconcerned by the details.

So, he'd been kidnapped by the Russians. That meant they'd risked flying into Austria to intercept him and blow away his chopper.

Whatever they wanted, someone with a higher rank than major would be asking the questions soon. The officer was obviously jumping the gun and trying to snitch a little glory for himself. Jack figured it wouldn't hurt to try to parlay that ambition into some solid information.

The major produced a doctor's black bag and began to prepare a set of hypodermic syringes. "When we are finished with you, you shall better appreciate the error of your ways."

"And you expect me to see the error of my ways when you transform me into a human pincushion. I suppose you want to be a doctor when you grow up."

Grimaldi's sarcasm was wasted on the plump, smug Russian, who said, "Forgive me. Mr. Grimaldi. I have not introduced myself. Major Engels, Doctor of Medicine, at your service." The last phrase blasted past his thick lips with a snort of laughter.

The doctor continued, "My specialty is seeing people like yourself through lengthy interrogations. It is not always easy to keep General Abovian's subjects healthy. You would be much wiser to talk now and save yourself a great deal of discomfort."

Jack saw his opportunity to find out the motive behind his abduction. "What do you want from me?"

"Everything, of course. Every operation you have flown for the enemy."

Jack knotted his brows to show that he was considering the major's proposition.

The KGB had him at their mercy behind the iron curtain. The pilot grinned wryly at the last thought. Mercy was the last thing they would show him. Then his face became serious again as he pondered his situation.

The United States wasn't going to send a strike force to get him out, but there was always the possibility that Hal Brognola could not prevent the President from sending someone to "put Jack out of his misery." There had been a lot of CIA assassinations recently to cover the extent of the President's covert operations in Central America.

Jack knew most of the Stony Man operations and would rather be killed than sing to the Russians.

Able Team could not try to help him. The defector was more important; they would not endanger her safety, even if they did know where to find him.

It was very tempting to buy time by giving this ambitious doctor false information. Jack knew he'd be granted a minor reprieve while it was being checked out. The difficulty would come in keeping his lies consistent. Jack doubted he could do it. Then there was the problem of the general. He'd probably be much brighter than the major. Starting to talk would be a mistake. Was there some way to get more information from the major before this Abovian character showed up?

"You'll get nothing from me, Major Engels. I'll be out of here before tomorrow," Grimaldi said smugly.

"Ah, of course. But that is precisely why you are here. You surely do not think we took all the trouble of setting up a defection just to kidnap you?"

Grimaldi frowned and the major noted the American's puzzlement. He hastened to explain.

"Oh, we shall gather whatever information you have for us. That is to be assumed. But you must have guessed by now that you are only bait."

"Bait! Who's the fish?"

"Colonel John Phoenix."

Grimaldi was determined to give nothing away. He knew the Russians had wanted Mack Bolan, whom they knew as Colonel John Phoenix, ever since their assault on Stony Man Farm. And they had succeeded in framing him for the execution of one of the Polish dissident leaders, but had been unable to keep their hands on Phoenix. Bolan had become an outlaw again, hunted by both the KGB and the CIA.

Grimaldi decided to play the game.

"I've heard of this Phoenix," Grimaldi began.

"Heard of him!" Engels exploded. "You are his personal pilot."

Didn't they know that the big warrior was on the Washington hit list? Grimaldi decided it wouldn't hurt to probe.

"I haven't flown him since he went over to your side," Grimaldi said in a cold voice.

Engels cocked an eyebrow and looked amused. "Ah yes, those delightful rumors that Colonel Phoenix is on the CIA's hit list. Surely you do not think we're stupid enough to believe that?"

"Why not? If you believed Karl Marx, you'll believe anything."

The major leaned across the desk until his face

was two inches from Jack's. "To say nothing of believing Lenin and Engels, my great-uncle, correct?"

"You said it."

"For your information, Mr. American Pilot, we knew that the transfer of an important defector would be too big a thing for Phoenix to miss. We waited until he was spotted in Vienna before going ahead with the defection. General Abovian himself went to Vienna to make sure the colonel picked up the right trail. Just before I came in here to talk to you, I had confirmation that John Phoenix is traveling in the general's car. The moment the car stops here, the colonel will be our prisoner. Do you understand?"

Grimaldi kept his face expressionless, but Engels's statement had rattled the pilot. Was it possible that Mack had been in Austria? Was this a hoax to loosen his tongue?

"You don't need any information from me if you already have this Phoenix character in the palm of your hand," Grimaldi said. His voice grated from tension.

"You will not get off that easily. What you give us will be compared with the information we get from Phoenix. You will both be most uncomfortable if you are lying."

Jack Grimaldi watched Dr. Engels as he carefully filled needles from small bottles capped with rubber stoppers.

"You say we are near Kosice?" Grimaldi asked.

"Yes, one of our new bases, just north of the industrial sector," Engels replied absentmindedly. He set down another syringe and looked speculatively at the pilot. "On this base we have the People's Museum of Aviation. Many of Europe's planes from World War I and earlier are here and many are in working order."

A glazed look appeared in Engels's eyes for a moment and Grimaldi guessed he was contemplating the might of the motherland. Then the doctor shook his head as he reined in his thoughts.

Engels picked up one of the needles, but before he could plunge it into Jack's arm, a telephone rang. The doctor grumbled as he walked over to the desk and lifted the receiver.

Even if Grimaldi could understand Russian, it would have done him little good. Engels did little more than grunt as he listened to the voice on the other end of the line. When he hung up the phone, his grin was humorless.

"It seems as if your Colonel Phoenix is bound to give us some trouble."

"But I don't—" Jack began.

Engels waved a hand in impatient dismissal. "There is little use wasting your time denying things we already know. Colonel Phoenix will be our prisoner in a very few moments. All your denials are useless."

Jack had a feeling that things had just gotten bleaker.

GENERAL LEOPOLD ABOVIAN kept his eyes closed and pretended to snooze. He would have preferred to keep his eyes on the American in the seat beside him, but wanted to be sure that he wouldn't gloat and give the game away before they were safely over the border into Czechoslovakia.

Once they crossed the frontier it would scarcely matter, but Phoenix would be allowed to think that he was in control until the car reached Kosice. However, six vehicles would alternate in boxing the general's car all the way there. Abovian hoped the border guards would not overdo their part and make his victim suspicious.

Normally, the KGB would not waste so many man-hours to capture one man, but Phoenix was a special case. Already that fool, Strakhov, had wasted many men in his personal vendetta with Phoenix. The fact that the American had killed Strakhov's son should not have blurred the major general's judgment.

It was a matter of face—the KGB had lost too much of it due to Strakhov's duel with Phoenix. Now Abovian found himself with the disagreeable job of trying to reestablish the KGB as a force to be feared, not snickered at.

Strakhov had taken the challenge of this warrior personally and met defeat after defeat. Abovian would not make the same mistake. He had mobilized Cuba to convene the Terrorism Limitation Conference, and to let slip that Wendy Pitt would defect from the conference. As a defector, Pitt was sufficiently important to attract the very best America had to offer.

Abovian had set up the kidnapping of the pilot and then offered himself as a ticket to the iron curtain, certain that the mysterious Colonel Phoenix would seize the opportunity. Abovian was content to play the game of cat and mouse. The American was lying about his identity. Surely he must know that the photos of John Phoenix had been circulated. Dostenko indeed.

The general had been surprised at how quickly Phoenix had reacted, but it didn't matter. All had been prepared ahead of time.

Abovian opened his eyes a slit and saw the American slipping Nicolai's gun into a side pocket. That meant they were approaching the border stations at Bratislava. It would be possible to take him now, but it would be foolish. Let the fish hook himself well before reeling him in.

The Austrians were cold and formal. They were still simmering over the Russian invasion of their airspace. The border patrol examined the three Russian passports, scowled at the diplomatic immunity and waved the Mercedes on to the Czech checkpoint.

The captain of the guard emerged from the border station and handled the car himself. He saluted smartly to Abovian and asked for papers. He appeared to give all three sets of papers a thorough examination and then handed them back.

The slow examination of the papers was designed to build tension in the car. If the American was worried, he certainly didn't show it. He looked as if the process bored him. Abovian had to admire the American's cool nerve. The captain saluted smartly once more and handed back the papers. Nicolai drove on.

The Soviet officer was careful not to look behind. He knew there would be a bread truck following them. He knew also that there was no bread in the truck; instead there were eight well-trained commandos. The truck would follow them through the rolling countryside to Nitra. There, a sedan with what appeared to be four tourists in it would take the place of the truck.

Ahead was a semitrailer, also full of commandos. It, too, would leapfrog with cars to prevent the American from knowing he was in a trap. There was always the chance he could be tricked into giving information while he still felt he was in control.

Abovian said, "Tell me, Colonel, what brings you to this part of the world?"

Bolan smiled. He admired the general's coolness, but was a touch worried by it. The general was more than cool; he behaved like a man who was enjoying himself. The trick was to find out which cards the general was hiding up his sleeve.

"You know what brings me here. The pilot you kidnapped."

Abovian made no attempt at denial, which added to Bolan's unease. If the general felt his life was at stake, Bolan had no doubt that Abovian would have no information about any missing pilot.

When Bolan revealed nothing else, the Russian army psychiatrist tried probing. "You realize that we must collect all the information that each of you can give us. It is necessary for the security of the state."

"I realize that you want information. I doubt its necessity to you."

"There is no need to doubt that, Colonel. Information is what this cold war of ours is all about. Do you not agree?"

Bolan smiled in reply. It was sufficient to goad Abovian into trying to continue the conversation.

"I have instructed one of our doctors to prepare Mr. Grimaldi for questioning. It is wonderful what medical science can do to keep you healthy, even under prolonged interrogation."

"Too bad. There'll be no interrogation this time."

Bolan cautiously checked the traffic both ahead of the general's Mercedes and behind it. He kept up the constant surveillance because it seemed to add to Nicolai's tension. The driver kept glancing at Bolan in his rearview mirror.

Abovian made several more attempts to draw Bolan into conversation, but with little result. The big warrior stayed alert and answered only when it suited him. Bolan did not waste energy trying to pump Abovian. He had no way of checking the accuracy of the answers.

The plan had worked this far: neither Abovian nor his driver had paused to wonder whether or not Bolan knew exactly where they were taking him.

At noon Bolan permitted a stop for gasoline, but no one was allowed out of the car. A rest stop was made at the side of the road where Bolan could keep his weapon out, concealed by the side of the car. They simply went without food or drink.

"You must be getting tired," Abovian remarked as they resumed the journey through Czechoslovakia.

Bolan said nothing.

From Nitra they had headed north through Topol'cany and past the woods of an immense hunting preserve. The foothills steepened and grain fields gave way to grazing cattle. The road became more dilapidated the farther they traveled from the Austrian border. Car and truck traffic lessened, bicycles and motorcycles increased.

They made good time. Bolan noted that the few police cars they spotted pointedly ignored the speeding Mercedes. As they approached Kosice, near the eastern rim of Czechoslovakia, Nicolai chose a highway running north. Bolan then knew where they were headed—the large Soviet army camp just north of a region of heavy industry.

Bolan waited until he spotted a narrow dirt track that ran off the highway, winding into the mountains. "Turn here," he commanded Nicolai.

The surprised aide paused, waiting for orders from Abovian. Bolan thumbed back the hammer on the Zastava. The tension in the car made the click sound as loud as a shot. Nicolai swung the car off the highway.

Bolan kept the gun ready and glanced back through the rear window.

"You are right, Colonel," Abovian said. "There are troops following us. We are now on a dead-end road. The moment we deviated from our route, the command car called for helicopter support. Do you not think it would be wise to surrender?''

5

Senator Andrew Pitt paced the tiled floor of the den at Stony Man Farm as he fought to contain his impatience.

The senator was not a tall man, but he was impressive. The gray didn't show in his light blond hair. His skin had the dark tan that comes only from long hours on salt water. At a hundred sixty-five pounds, he was slightly overweight, but it didn't show on his sturdy frame.

Standing at the entrance to the room, Lao Ti could see some of the magnetism that made Pitt one of the few senators who weren't worried about being reelected. He looked up abruptly when Ti glided into the room.

She stood five feet six inches. Her straight black hair was cropped just below the ears, at the nape of the neck. She wore no makeup and her face bore the features of her Vietnamese mother. She wore a plaid shirt and a pair of tight jeans.

If Senator Pitt had not been a friend of the President and had not been told some of Ti's background, he would have thought her to be a college girl. It was hard to believe that this small woman, brought up and educated in Japan, had a doctorate in physics and was perhaps the most able computer scientist to emigrate to America.

"Your daughter is safe, Senator," Ti said. Her voice calmed him.

"How do you know? What happened?"

"Able Team contacted us from Venice. They're boarding a military jet bound for Andrews Air Force Base at this moment. Your secretary telephoned. She asked me to tell you that Zachery Jones will be able to keep your three-o'clock appointment."

The news startled Pitt. He glanced hurriedly at his watch, his expression changing rapidly from annoyance to agony to determination.

Pitt said, "Please have my pilot warm up my plane at once. I must be in Florida in time to prepare for that appointment. I'll send the pilot back for my daughter."

Lao Ti stared speculatively at the senator. If Pitt had expected her to make some objection about the importance of meeting a daughter he had not seen since she was three, or about putting off the appointment, he did not know Lao Ti.

She said only, "I'll see to it."

Lao left the room and proceeded to the communications center where she knew she'd find Hal Brognola, Stony Man's direct liaison with the President. She was aware that Hal would not stray far from the center until more information could be gathered about the fate of Jack Grimaldi.

"I'm to get Senator Pitt's pilot to our strip immediately. He's decided to keep a prior appointment, rather than wait for his daughter. Do you need me here, Hal?''

Brognola glanced sharply at the diminutive Oriental. "What do you have in mind?"

"The finger of coincidence is attached to the hand of an illusionist," Lao answered.

"So?"

"So I wish to see what forgotten appointment has suddenly become more important than seeing a daughter who was kidnapped from him when she was three, and whom he is not supposed to have seen since."

Brognola chewed on his unlit cigar before saying, "You're right, it's an interesting coincidence. One of the Air Force training jets should get you to the New Tamiami Airport at least half an hour before his plane can arrive."

Lao nodded her acknowledgment and began dialing the number to order an Air Force jet on standby.

THE ROAR OF THE FOUR Pratt & Whitney turbofan engines slowly receded into the background as the Boeing VC-137 gained altitude over the Italian Alps. Lyons returned from the communications center located between the cockpit and the conference room. The rear section of the 137B was set up as a passenger liner.

Lyons perched on the arm of a seat on the aisle across from Wendy Pitt and Blancanales.

"Hal was shook up when I told him the Russians had captured Jack. He'll do what he can, but it looks bad."

From where he was stretched out on two seats, Gadgets spoke up. "The big guy will find Jack."

Lyons shook his head.

Blancanales put into words what both he and Lyons were thinking. "Mack no longer has any organization behind him. How's he even going to manage to find where they took Jack?"

"I don't know," Gadgets replied. "I've never known how he was going to do half the stuff he did. Like us, he'll do what must be done."

"Who is this person you speak of?" Wendy Pitt asked.

"He used to be in charge of our operation. Now he's on his own. You almost met him in Stadtpark," Blancanales explained.

The blonde blinked a few times and seemed confused. She looked at Carl Lyons who was still resting his hip on the seat arm opposite her.

"In the park, when I was being hurried away, I looked back. You stopped someone from shooting me. Is that the one?"

Lyons nodded.

Wendy shuddered. Politician put an arm around her shoulder.

"What's wrong?" Pol asked.

"One man tried to kill me when I come to you people. Now I find out he is a friend of yours."

"He will not harm you," Pol assured her.

She looked into the dark eyes of the white-haired man beside her. "I believe you," she whispered.

6

Bolan ignored Abovian's suggestion that the Executioner surrender.

The side road was nothing more than ruts in the dirt. Nicolai drove cautiously on the primitive trail.

"Nicolai," Bolan said, "a truck and a car are following us. Leave them a mile behind and you live. Fail to buy me that much time and I'll shoot you."

Nicolai's only response was to push the accelerator to the floor. Both Bolan and Abovian braced themselves against the rough ride.

"It is no use, Colonel," Abovian shouted between jolts. "This lane will end and you shall have to surrender eventually."

Bolan squeezed the trigger of the Zastava. One 9mm slug cored Abovian's left eye. It exited from a two-inch hole in the back of his skull and smashed into the side window behind the general. A spray of blood and brains decorated the glass and the interior of the luxury car.

"Turn the car around, stop, then get my bag from the trunk," Bolan commanded.

Nicolai was pale as he glanced at the remains of

his superior. He did as Bolan ordered and when they stepped out of the car, they could hear the truck laboring up the grade. It was closing in. Bolan snatched his bag and opened it.

"Start the car, then leave," he barked.

The Russian driver wasted no time trying to guess what the strange American had in mind. He took off into the nearby woods, glancing over his shoulder as he ran.

Bolan produced a handful of C-4 from the bag and wrapped it around a percussion primer. Then he stuck the explosive to the front bumper of the car. He set the emergency brake, put the automatic shift into Drive, and stood beside the driver's seat, waiting.

A few seconds later the bread truck appeared over a rise in the trail.

Bolan released the emergency brake and ran back for his bag. He snatched it on the run and dived behind a boulder.

The Mercedes headed back downhill. The concussive force of the explosion hurled the two vehicles into the air. Even with his eyes closed Bolan could discern the brightness of the blast. Shards of metal rained down as far as the warrior's position, and he hugged the boulder for protection.

Amid the metallic drumming of flying fragments, Bolan heard loud thuds, and he opened his eyes to see bodies of soldiers landing on the ground.

Bolan sprang back to his feet and sprinted toward the wreck. The fragments were still tumbling down through branches.

The Executioner's left fist was wrapped around the Zastava. His right fist wielded a Heckler & Koch MP-5K machine pistol, snatched from his war bag.

Even though it had only a 4 1/2-inch barrel, the MP-5K was as accurate as an Uzi. The MP pumped 9mm parabellums at 900 rounds per minute.

The few dazed survivors of the explosion stumbled out of the back of the bread truck. Confused and shaken, they were milling about in the smoke of the blast like blind men. Bolan's MP-5K chattered its message of death and soldiers performed a grisly dance in the smoky swirls.

The black Zil limousine had managed to stop before plowing into the back of the truck. Four young men sprang from it. Three had Makarovs in their right hands; the fourth brandished a submachine gun. They raked the trees with SMG fire, hoping for a lucky strike, but the warrior had already left that firezone and faded into the woods.

He threw away the empty Yugoslavian automatic and stripped to his blacksuit, then raced through the bush toward the highway.

The silenced Beretta clung to its accustomed spot under his left arm and the AutoMag rode his hip. The MP-5K was once again in the Executioner's right fist. Ammunition and explosives hugged his waist on a web belt, each item within easy reach. The empty war bag and civilian clothing had been left behind. Such items could be acquired again at need.

Bolan moved quietly ahead of the pursuers, calculating his path to meet the highway where the Mercedes had turned off.

The Executioner had spotted Abovian's trap as soon as it had closed in. Once he saw the four men in the Zil, it had been easy to tab the other vehicles that had stayed with them for a number of miles. The almost mechanical rotation of vehicles had not helped Abovian's plans.

Bolan had been unwilling to drive straight into the enemy camp boxed by enemy troops. But now that he'd pried the box open, it was time to find Grimaldi.

An easy jog through the woods brought the Executioner back to the place where he had forced Nicolai to turn off the highway onto the trail.

A military command car stood blocking the end of the trail. Four men surrounded Nicolai, and they failed to notice Bolan's approach until it was too late.

Two soldiers released Nicolai and tried to swing up their Kalashnikovs to meet the intruder.

A 3-round burst from the MP-5K aerated the brains of the smaller soldier, and another slug high in the right shoulder spun his companion into the path of a second 9mm mangler.

The commanding officer, a colonel, had his side arm halfway from its holster when a 3-round burst tore out his windpipe and a two-inch section of spine. The fourth man, an NCO, dropped his weapon and raised his hands.

Bolan sighed. He couldn't leave enemy troops at his back, but his war wasn't with the soldiers, it was with the Communist-party hacks who turned these patriotic citizens into menaces to the freedom of both other countries and their own.

The warrior looked at Nicolai, who hadn't moved. Resignation had stamped his face to a tired blankness.

Bolan asked a question by raising a brow and nodding to the two bodies at Nicolai's feet.

"They wanted to know why I was alive if the general was dead," the Russian explained in hoarse English.

"What did you tell them?"

A trace of a smirk appeared in the corner of the aide's mouth, then quickly disappeared. "I said that the brave general tried to take you bare-handed before I could get close. That you shot him. So I felt it was my duty to stay alive and report."

Bolan bent down and started to undress the taller soldier, the one he had hit in the shoulder before killing.

"Stick to the story. It might get you by. Does he speak English?" Bolan asked, indicating the man with arms upraised.

"Yes, but you shall get nothing from him."

Bolan pulled on the soldier's uniform over his combat suit, switching the SMG from hand to hand as he did so. The two surviving Russians were being careful not to make any sudden moves.

"What's the name of the doctor who's questioning the American pilot?" Bolan asked.

"Major Engels."

"Drive me to him."

"He's inside the army camp. You cannot go there."

"Drag those bodies out of sight and let's get going."

The two Russians shrugged at the madness of the American and hastened to keep him in an agreeable mood. When the bodies were out of sight of the road, Bolan climbed into the right rear seat and gestured for the two Russians to get into the front.

Nicolai pulled the car onto the road and started driving just as three helicopters swooped in overhead. The numbers were falling quickly. Bolan knew that the Russians would have things figured out very soon.

"Faster," he told Nicolai.

The driver shrugged as he stepped on the accelerator. "They'll stop us at the gate. All vehicles must stop at the gate."

"By all means," Bolan agreed, "stop at the gate."

JACK GRIMALDI WAS EXPERIENCING anguish far more intense than any pain the Russians could cause. The trouble was, he knew too much. The moment Dr. Engels administered those drugs, there was no way that Grimaldi could prevent himself from exposing Able Team.

It was ironic that he didn't know Mack Bolan's current whereabouts and could only provide history on the big guy.

Jack fought down his panic and assessed his situation. He took a deep breath and forced himself to look at his surroundings. His arms and legs were securely bound to a wooden armchair.

Major Engels seemed to hold all the cards. Again, Jack glanced at the arms of the chair. It was not built strong, but was more than he could pull apart. Jack's mind had begun to function. He must stall until his plan was better formed.

"Major Engels, when was the last time you had a woman? I heard a story about Russian officers sent to these remote outposts. You know, after a while they don't care to consort with women. And it's not surprising, the way your women look."

Engels paused, perplexed, the confusion changing to new fury.

"Are you suggesting—" the major, a man some twenty years married, began.

Grimaldi began to laugh in the Russian's face until a huge fist caught him on the side of the head and sent the chair off-balance. The Stony pilot threw his energy into twisting on the ropes, causing the chair to crash down on the corner of one of the arms, smashing it at the joints.

With the lightning reflexes that made Grimaldi one of America's crack flying aces, he pushed with his free hand against the floor, twisting the chair up and down onto the other arm, managing to break it off also. Now his arms were free, though still tied to the chair.

Snarling with rage, Engels aimed a kick at the pilot. Grimaldi fielded the kick with a chair arm, bringing the other arm in behind the Russian's knee.

A sudden pressure and the major fell on top of Grimaldi. He grabbed his belt, jerked, moved an arm up under the chin and the other chair arm behind the neck. He squeezed.

The telephone started to ring. Jack held the frantically struggling doctor while the phone rang and rang. Soon they would send somebody to investigate why Engels was not answering.

7

The command car approached the gate, and Bolan snapped at the two Russians in the front seat. "If either of you tries to alert the guards, you both die."

A uniformed corporal approached the vehicle from the right side, while another kept a machine gun trained on its occupants from the left. The first sentry noticed Bolan's bloody jacket, but did not comment on it.

"Your papers," the man demanded.

Bolan slurred his speech as if he was weak from loss of blood. "I carry personal orders from General Abovian to Major Engels. He is to attend to my shoulder while I report."

"Your documents." The guard held out his hand.

"Corporal, you are wasting time. The message is of utmost importance and if it is not delivered, you shall have to answer to the general," Bolan replied, reaching into his jacket as if searching for his ID. His fingers grasped the butt of the silenced 93-R.

The corporal hesitated a few seconds more, then stepped back and waved them through.

"Drive slowly around the perimeter of the camp," Bolan ordered the driver as soon as they were out of sight of the gate.

"I can see why General Abovian thought you were such a dangerous opponent," Nicolai commented as he took a right-hand fork in the compound's dusty road. "I was certain no authorized person could penetrate this base."

"The troops are all armed," Bolan observed.

The two Russians in the front seat exchanged puzzled looks. The NCO spoke for the first time. "This is a base of the Russian army and air force. Of course soldiers have weapons."

"While on base?"

"We are not in Russia." The man's voice was frosty.

Bolan did not need to probe further as he reasoned it out for himself. Russian troops were stationed in Czechoslovakia, Hungary and Poland, but that did not mean they were welcome.

Although the Warsaw Pact countries were supposed to be allies, the Russians had to maintain a constant state of alert on their foreign bases.

Large rectangular buildings flanked the airstrip on three sides. It was located at the end of the compound farthest from the main gate.

Three MiGs and two gunships clustered around one of the structures, marking it as a hangar.

Bolan could not determine the purpose of the other two buildings. They might have been additional hangars, but there were no aircraft outside them and the doors were closed. One building should represent all the hangar space needed by a detachment of this size, Bolan reasoned.

As they moved back toward the gate along the other side of the compound, Bolan began to ask questions. "Where's the officers' mess?"

Nicolai jerked a thumb toward a three-story building near the center of the compound. "Your uniform does not entitle you to eat there."

Nicolai's humor alerted Bolan. The general's aide was no longer behaving as a hostage.

"Where are they holding the pilot?" Bolan demanded.

"We have no facilities to detain people in a camp on foreign soil. Detainees are either shipped to the motherland immediately or turned over to the local army or police. Your pilot is being questioned in General Abovian's office."

"Take me there."

"As you wish, Colonel."

The car continued in the same direction. Bolan pressed the Beretta's silencer to the back of Nicolai's head.

"And make sure it's the right office." Bolan's voice left no doubt of his intentions.

Nicolai pushed the accelerator down harder. The command car sped toward a two-story building flying Russian and Czech flags.

"When we stop, you two come in with me," Bolan instructed.

Nicolai brought the command car to a halt at the front entrance. Bolan had the Heckler & Koch subgun in his left hand pointed steadily at the two

Russians. The sleek Beretta was in his right fist. They got out of the car slowly, as if they were stiff.

"No more stalling or you get a bullet. Get me into that office and you're free to go."

The soldiers hurried into the building and met no resistance.

Abovian's office was on the first floor. The two Russians led Bolan along a deserted corridor. They heard scuffling sounds inside the office.

"Break down the door," Bolan commanded.

The Russians threw their shoulders against the door in a halfhearted way. It held. Bolan's boot flashed past them and impacted just beside the knob. The doorjamb splintered and the door flew in. Bolan shoved the two Russians into the room and moved in after them.

As the soldiers staggered to regain balance, Bolan could see two figures on the floor, struggling. Before he could reach them, there was a snapping sound and the one in a Russian officer's uniform went limp.

Jack Grimaldi grinned up at Bolan. Outside, a siren began to wail.

"Perfect timing, Mack," Grimaldi told Bolan.

Bolan's Beretta disappeared into his shoulder rig and he drew out the Maringer knife from its forearm sheath. The blade flashed four times and the ropes fell from Grimaldi's arms and legs. Grimaldi dashed to the window.

"Couple of jeeploads of Ruskies pulling outside," the pilot reported.

"Anything we should know?" Bolan asked Nicolai, prodding him with the knife.

"There are checkpoints within the base that are not marked. You must stop and identify yourself."

Bolan nodded. "Okay. Leave."

The two Russians looked at him suspiciously, sure it was a trick.

Bolan knew he was increasing his risk by letting the two go, but his war was not with them. If he took life needlessly, he would be no better than the cannibals he was fighting. The two Russians slowly backed toward the exit, then turned and bolted.

The moment they gained the corridor, they were cut down by a hail of automatic-weapon fire from Russian troops.

Bolan snatched up the remains of the broken chair and heaved it through the window. Grimaldi was a split second behind the chair, diving through the window. Bolan followed on the pilot's heels.

Outside, the wail of the siren seemed much louder. Troops ran in all directions, but with a minimum of confusion. To Bolan's surprise, none of them seemed to be headed directly toward the Americans' position.

"Which way's the airstrip?" Grimaldi asked.

"There," Bolan said, indicating the hangar. Then he pointed to the three-story building in the middle of the compound. "But we want to go there first."

Grimaldi wasted no time on questions. He sprinted for the closest building between them and their objective. Bolan stayed on his heels, occasionally glancing back for sign of any pursuers.

The two warriors reached the end of a long barracks building. Soldiers were still pouring out the doors, clutching Kalashnikov rifles.

No one seemed to be concerned with the two men running toward them. Bolan spared no time guessing at reasons as he and Grimaldi sprinted into the building, forcing their way through the stream of exiting soldiers.

Bolan knew that soon he must get rid of the bloodstained jacket. Once the guard at the gate reported, the troops would be looking for it. He was still puzzled by how few soldiers searched for the two of them.

"Where are we headed?" Grimaldi asked.

"The officers' mess."

The two Americans strode into the mess building, deserted now, all the occupants having rushed out in answer to the wailing siren. Bolan took the stairs three at a time with Grimaldi following closely.

As they stepped from the stairwell into the hall, Bolan collided with a huge man in a flight suit who was running down the hall with a Kalashnikov. At the sight of the two intruders, the weapon automatically came up to firing position.

The Russian pilot was too close to the Executioner for any move to be effective, and Bolan brought his own subgun crashing against the Russian's temple. The man collapsed.

Bolan stripped the man of his colonel's uniform

while Grimaldi stood watch, the Kalashnikov in his hands. It took Bolan less than ninety seconds to discard the bloody army fatigues and put the flight clothing on over his black combat suit.

Bolan kicked open a door to one of the officer's rooms, walked over to the window and looked out. It suddenly became apparent why no one had paid any attention to them.

The base was well organized and the commander sharp. As far as Bolan could see, troops guarded the perimeter of the base.

The warrior realized that the maneuver had been rehearsed many times. Each man knew exactly where to position himself in order to seal off the base. Soon, they would be moving in for the building-to-building search, but the siren had been the signal to first block all escape routes.

"Let's get out of here before the search starts," he told Grimaldi.

They took the stairs two at a time. They ran out the front door right into the path of an armored troop carrier disgorging a search party of a dozen men.

THE MCDONNELL-DOUGLAS F-15B Eagle touched down on the west runway of the New Tamiami Airport. The Air Force pilot taxied to a remote corner of the field where he could await clearance for the return flight to Andrews Air Force Base.

Lao Ti looked at her watch, figuring she had almost another hour before Senator Pitt's private jet landed.

The pilot popped the canopy, then turned and spoke to her. "This is a civilian field, so there won't be any steps. It's a six-foot drop from the wings to the ground."

"No problem," Lao answered. She opened the double restraint harness and boosted herself out of the cockpit onto the top of the intake cowling. The pilot gasped when Lao jumped backward off the cowling. She grabbed the leading edge with her hands, hung for a second and then dropped to the ground.

The last the pilot saw of her, she was jauntily walking toward a hangar.

Lao had no trouble finding a place to stash her flight suit and emerged from a hangar five minutes later, just in time to see the F-15B Eagle clawing its way into the sky.

Lao threw her large handbag over one shoulder and started to walk toward the passenger terminal where she hoped to rent a car.

She had not taken five paces when a bright yellow Ferrari came through a gate and roared toward her.

Lao paused to determine whether the driver was aiming at her. The car swerved at the last moment and pulled up beside Lao.

The driver was in his twenties, blond. The blue eyes that looked directly into Lao's seemed to hold genuine interest in what they saw, and the smiling mouth held no hint of petulance.

"You must be Lao Ti. I'm Stew Williams. Hal Brognola said you'd need a good car for a tail job."

Lao stopped still. The man knew her name and knew enough to mention Hal Brognola. Either he was genuine or he would have to be eliminated. Despite these thoughts, she could not restrain a smile.

"A bright yellow Ferrari?"

"Sure. No one in his right mind would tail in a yellow Ferrari. No one will ever suspect you of trying."

"Why are you so certain I'm the one you're looking for?"

"I asked Mr. Brognola how to recognize you. He told me to look for a small Oriental woman disembarking from a military jet."

"You're not with the Justice Department," Lao said. It was not a question.

"How do you know?"

"I work with computers. I know the files."

"I'm with the Company."

"I don't need a Company man along on this."

"Lady, you don't have a Company man along on *this*, whatever *this* is. I'm just an errand boy."

"So it's the CIA who thinks a bright yellow Ferrari is the ideal car for tailing a suspect?"

Williams's fair skin took on a slight touch of red. He nodded, but didn't speak.

"Thank you. I'll take it."

Lao stepped closer to the Ferrari. She reached into her handbag and placed a small box on the car roof. In a moment she was bringing in the control tower. She could now monitor landing instructions, and she would be able to tell when the senator's plane was landing and on what part of the field.

"How do you get back?" Lao asked.

"Someone's waiting at the gate."

"And when I'm finished with the car?"

"Leave it at this parking lot. It'll be picked up."

"Thank you." Lao turned her back on Williams and dismissed him from her mind.

Pitt's plane made better time than Lao had expected. She was waiting outside the gates when the senator's car whipped past. The chauffeur-driven limo was easy to tail. Lao was beginning to believe the CIA reasoning that no one would expect to be tailed by the most conspicuous car on the road.

They traveled to the South Dixie Highway, then exited onto the Rickenbacker Causeway, a toll road that took them onto Key Biscayne.

Finally Pitt's car turned onto a small drive leading to a private marina just south of Crandon Park, on the bay side of the key. A guard at the gate was stopping cars and demanding to see membership cards.

Lao was forced to park on a residential street half a mile away and enter the marina by climbing the chain-link fence. She dropped safely on the far side of the fence. It was then a simple matter to wander around the marina.

Pitt's boat was called *Wendy III*. For Lao, the name added a further touch of mystery to the senator's actions.

Here was a man who named his yacht after a

daughter who had been kidnapped from him when she was three. Yet when she was finally released, he would not wait to meet her but came dashing back to Florida to take a trip in his yacht. Lao could make no sense of it.

The senator, his chauffeur and bodyguard all strode directly to the yacht as soon as the car was parked. Lao Ti saw the three-man crew on deck spring into action as soon as Pitt approached. Obviously they had been standing by, ready to be under way the minute he arrived.

Lao had two choices. She could find a charter yacht or helicopter and try to follow *Wendy III*. But she figured that by the time arrangements were made, it would be unlikely she'd find the yacht again. She would have to settle for waiting at the marina for its return and try to pick up the trail from there. She decided to report to Hal Brognola and settle down for a wait. But it irked her that she might never find out what was out at sea that was more important to Pitt than seeing his long-lost daughter.

8

Bolan reacted to the appearance of Russian troops by immediately taking command.

"The intruder has shown up at the airstrip. Move quickly," Bolan ordered in Russian.

Grimaldi climbed into the observer's seat behind the driver, and Bolan herded the soldiers back into the cramped rear section of the BTR-60 troop carrier, then forced his way inside among the men. With the top armor down, the troops had to duckwalk to their benches. Bolan and twelve Russian soldiers were crowded into a twelve-by-six-foot space that was only four feet high.

As the carrier lurched away, a noncommissioned officer said in a loud voice, "Comrade Colonel, I have not seen you on the base before. What is your name, please?"

Bolan did not miss the way the soldier was trying to slide his Kalashnikov from his shoulder in the cramped quarters.

The Executioner wasted no time with explanations. He slid the machine pistol from under his jacket. He silently offered up thanks for the 4 1/2-inch barrel.

The NCO was still trying to bring his assault

rifle low enough to shoot when the machine pistol stuttered once. Lead grains entered below the sternum and exited through the left shoulder blade, carrying most of the heart with it.

The soldier behind the NCO had twisted his head to determine the source of the noise. He was in time to get a face full of pulverized heart and other gore. The parabellum bullet tore into his left eye socket on its way to his brain.

Bolan set the MP-5K on single-shot mode before he fired again. Inside the metal walls, the tiny subgun made cannon-sized noises.

Troops shoved and pushed to bring their weapons to bear, but they were too confined to do so. One man near the front managed to draw a small backup gun. Bolan stopped him with a well-placed round. But the soldier stayed in his seat, unable to fall due to the press of bodies around him.

In fifteen seconds the clip in the MP-5K was as dead as the twelve Russian soldiers in the back of the troop carrier. Bolan braced himself against a side wall while he changed magazines, careful not to slip in the blood that covered the floor of the carrier.

In front, the driver heard the sound of bullets striking the steel armor between the observer and the troop compartment. He took his foot off the accelerator and twisted around to look at Grimaldi.

Grimaldi placed the tip of the Kalashnikov's barrel against the driver's temple. The foot went back down on the accelerator.

When they reached the airstrip, the driver braked the troop carrier to a sudden stop and turned to smirk at Grimaldi. Jack took his attention from the driver's face long enough to study the field.

The Russian troops not only guarded the perimeter of the base against escape, but also kept a large contingent around the planes. A hangar, three MiGs and two Hinds each had a machine gun emplacement nearby. Two companies of infantry patrolled the area.

When Bolan felt the carrier stop, he climbed out and, in plain sight of the troops guarding the airfield, walked to the front of the carrier. Both the driver's and observer's hatches were open.

Bolan quickly took in the situation at the landing strip. He needed a diversion. He leaned over the hatch, as if giving the driver instructions.

The driver watched in fascinated horror as the colonel unbuttoned his shirt and removed a detonation wire from a pocket in some kind of black underwear that he wore under the shirt. A radio detonator and remote-control unit came from another pocket. The madman in the Russian airforce uniform placed the three objects on top of the troop carrier. Then he picked up the cord and waved it in the driver's face.

"Do you know what this is?" he demanded.

The driver tried to swallow, but his mouth was too dry. Unable to speak, he forced himself to nod.

The Russian's horror froze him into place when

the big colonel smiled and threaded the det cord through the radio-activated detonator. Then he tied the wire and detonator around the driver's neck. It wasn't tight enough to choke him, but there was no way he could slide it off.

Then the maniac spoke again. "This thing has a range of one kilometer. As long as you drive through the fence and straight ahead, I'll have no reason to push this button." He waved the sending unit under the driver's nose. The man nearly fainted, waiting for a finger to accidentally touch the switch.

While Bolan was explaining to the driver how the game was played, Grimaldi climbed from the carrier. The curiosity and suspicion on the faces of the troops on the airfield made the pilot wary.

Bolan stepped back and told the sweating driver, "Go. Now!"

The big engine of the BTR-60 howled its protest as it accelerated toward the chain-link fence.

"Astanofka! Astanofka!" Bolan yelled.

Grimaldi whipped up the Kalashnikov and fired a shot at the retreating vehicle.

The attention of the troops swung away from Bolan and Grimaldi and centered on the troop carrier. When it became apparent that the armored vehicle wasn't going to stop, other automatic-weapon fire began to rake its steel plate. The vehicle crashed through the fence and kept on going.

Bolan and Grimaldi turned and walked away quickly, careful not to draw the attention of the soldiers from the vehicle.

"One of these buildings should be a museum for old planes," Grimaldi explained to Bolan. "If we can slip in without being noticed, those antiques might be our ticket out of here."

Bolan was unsure how old planes could escape from MiGs and gunships, but he trusted Grimaldi's judgment in anything to do with flying. He watched the troop carrier disappear over the brow of a hill, and asked, "Which of the two buildings?"

"Dunno. Let's try the closest."

The two warriors walked into the nearest prefab shed.

The building was the base armory. The entrance area was separated from the storage area by a heavy mesh screen. In the middle of the screened wall was an opening over a long counter.

Soldiers were waving requisitions at a supply officer and two harried clerks. In one corner of the reception area, trying to stay out of the way of the mob, stood three guards. Bolan glared at them until they snapped to attention. He started to stride toward the counter when Grimaldi plucked at his sleeve.

"Mack, over there! Those are SAMs and launchers. If those missiles have the new cryogenic nose, we could use four." Grimaldi spoke in a low whisper.

"You serious?" Bolan asked, then let his voice go on in louder Russian.

"MiGs and Hinds are too heavily guarded. If we get an old plane to fly, those SAMs would be our best defence," Grimaldi said.

Bolan strode over to the counter and grabbed the supply officer by the arm. "We pounded on the truck-bay door for ten minutes. What is the matter with you?" he demanded.

"We have been busy, sir."

"Send one of your clerks with me, now," Bolan insisted.

The man turned and barked an order to one of the clerks and then turned back to Bolan. "If you go around to the door now, sir . . ."

Bolan vaulted the counter. "We shall follow this man. We won't stand outside another ten minutes." Grimaldi slid over the counter, too. The officer opened his mouth to protest, closed it again, shrugged and went back to work.

Bolan halted the clerk at the rack of four-foot-long missiles. "Take this with you," Bolan commanded, thrusting an SA-7 launcher into the clerk's hands. He then stooped and easily swung to his shoulder a box containing four of the missiles. The clerk's eyes bulged, as each missile weighed about twenty-three pounds.

"Your . . . your requisition, sir?"

"The truck driver has it, imbecile. I'm simply saving time and obeying my orders as you are."

The clerk nodded glumly and led the way to the loading bay. When he opened the door, there was no truck in sight.

"There he is now," Bolan said as a truck came toward them. "Bring me an RPD and four drums of ammunition. That also is on the driver's requisition."

The clerk looked nervously at Bolan, set down the launcher and hastily went to comply with the order.

The truck was backing into the loading zone when the clerk returned, staggering with the heavy machine gun and the box of clips. While Grimaldi accepted the awkward load, Bolan slashed downward with the edge of his palm, paralyzing the man and rendering him unconscious. The clerk slumped backward into Bolan's arms. The Executioner dragged the body to an unused area and left it concealed under a tarpaulin.

When the driver got out of the truck, Grimaldi and Bolan were walking out of the truck bay, each carrying a load of weapons.

Bolan grunted at the driver. "The supply clerk is helping me with a rush order. He'll be right back to look after you." Bolan hoped the deceit would have the Russians looking for the supply clerk outside the armory.

There was only one building left that could have housed the antique planes. Grimaldi and Bolan trudged across the concrete adjacent to the landing strip with their heavy loads. None of the numerous troops thought to stop and question them.

Grimaldi placed his load on the ground and tried the first door they came to. It was locked, but he borrowed Bolan's knife and had the door open in less than a minute. He returned Bolan's knife and picked up the machine gun and ammo. Bolan set down his own load just inside the door and shut and locked it behind them. Grimaldi flicked on the light switch. When the harsh glare of the overhead bare bulbs filled the building, Grimaldi sucked in his breath.

About twenty planes, all from the first quarter of the century, were crammed into the hangar. Most were in good condition, having been reconstructed as closely as practical to the original plane and put in flying order.

Grimaldi did not realize that he was humming as he wandered around planes, touching, standing back to admire, peering into cockpits.

Bolan relaxed momentarily as he watched Grimaldi dancing around the planes. Jack might have been enjoying himself, but he had not forgotten business. Bolan noticed that Grimaldi's seemingly aimless wandering was narrowing down to fewer and fewer airplanes.

"It'll have to be this one, the Lloyd C-II," Grimaldi finally announced. "And look, there are even a couple pairs of goggles. Probably left here to add authenticity. In any case, the Lloyd seems to have flown recently and has a slightly smaller engine."

"A smaller engine?"

Grimaldi nodded. He waved an arm to indicate all the planes. "Nothing in here is going to outrun a MiG. We'll have to hedgehop all the way, below radar, and hope we're not spotted. The smaller and cooler the engine, the more missileproof we are."

Bolan understood. The Russians used two types

of air-to-air missiles: heat seekers and radar guided. The smaller, cooler engine would probably not run warmly enough for a heat-seeking missile to latch onto it. The cloth-and-wood construction of the plane would not reflect radar, only the metal parts would. So the smaller engine was a bonus and not a drawback, although it was slow.

"I've got to check out the engine and get us fueled up," Grimaldi said.

"What can I do, Jack?"

"Try to find a way to lash the SAMs and launcher to the struts. You decide what you need. I'll be busy with the engine."

"How are we going to use a surface-to-air missile launcher in one of these firetraps? The back-blast will turn us into a flying bonfire."

"When you want to shoot, you'll have to tap me on the shoulder to indicate direction. These light craft will do a U-turn in a quarter mile. A fast MiG takes twenty to thirty miles to make the return run, depending on the speed."

"You make it sound as if we've got all the advantages."

Grimaldi grinned. "Not quite. They can either come in at their slowest possible speed with flaps up and landing gear down and try to machine-gun us, or they can simply come in at full speed and kick the whole damn crate apart with air turbulence."

"And you think we have a chance in the Lloyd?"

"Better than fifty-fifty."

"Let's get busy. I'll start with those SAMs."

"Double-check that they're all the updated type with the cryogenic heads."

Bolan paused. "What's that?"

"The early SAMs weren't sensitive enough to lock onto a jet from anything but the rear and weren't fast enough to catch up to a MiG. The new ones have cooled heads so that the heat sensors can penetrate them. They can now lock onto a jet from the front or rear."

Bolan opened the case and peered at the missiles. "They seem to be the right ones."

"Some tools in the bench in this corner. Let's go."

Bolan agonized for half an hour, trying to find a way to fit the four-foot missiles in the cramped quarters of the small plane and still be able to draw them and load the launcher. Nothing seemed to work. In frustration he walked around the hangar. In one corner he found some wire.

"Jack, what happens if I make a pocket outside the plane and put the missiles and launcher in that—sort of a quiver for the Russian arrows?"

Grimaldi peered around the cowling. "No problem. Men used to ride on the wings of these crates. Just make it fast. We want to take off tonight."

Bolan found some light wood and hastily constructed a form that would fit over the four missiles and launchers. If they ever went into a power dive he would have to put his hands over the opening to keep the warheads from falling out.

When he had tacked the form together, Bolan

picked up the missiles and launcher and shoved them inside the rear cockpit out of sight, an almost instinctive move of a battle-wary mind.

Then Bolan tacked the form to the side of the plane and lashed it to the fuselage with wire. He twisted the final length of wire around the elongated wooden frame and was about to glue fiberglass cloth over the structure when the door opened and a sergeant backed by four armed guards charged into the hangar.

DYNAMITE OFFER

4 EXPLOSIVE NOVELS PLUS SUNGLASSES FREE

delivered right to your home with no obligation to buy — ever

Mean up your act with these tough sunglasses

Unbeatable! That's the word for these tough street-smart shades. Durable metal frame. Scratch-resistant acrylic lenses. Fold 'em into a zip pouch and tuck 'em in your pocket. Best of all, they're yours free.

FREE BOOKS & SUNGLASSES

YEAH, send my 4 **free** Gold Eagle novels plus my **free** sunglasses. Then send me 6 brand-new Gold Eagle novels (2 **Mack Bolans** and one each of **Phoenix Force, Able Team, Track** and **SOBs**) every second month as they come off the presses. Bill me at the low price of $1.95 each (for a total of $11.70 per shipment—a saving of $2.30 off the retail price). There are no shipping, handling or other hidden charges. I can always return a shipment and cancel at any time. Even if I never buy a book from Gold Eagle, the 4 free books and the sunglasses (a $6.95 value) are mine to keep.

166 CIM PAGM

NAME_____

ADDRESS_____ APT._____

CITY_____

STATE_____ ZIP_____

Offer limited to one per household and not valid for present subscribers. Prices subject to change.

PRINTED IN U.S.A.

JOIN FORCES WITH GOLD EAGLE'S HEROES

- Mack Bolan...lone crusader against the Mafia and KGB
- Able Team...3-man combat squad blitzes global terrorism
- Phoenix Force...5 mercenaries battle international crime
- Track...weapons genius stalks madman around the world
- SOBs...avengers of justice from Vietnam to Iran

For free offer, detach and mail

9

The morning after the ruckus in Stadtpark, Colonel Fernandez Maceo, leader of the Cuban delegation to the Terrorism Limitation Conference, requested the floor as soon as the meeting began.

He denounced the American terrorist activities that resulted in the deaths of two Cuban nationals and the kidnapping of a third. He demanded that America immediately return the kidnap victim, one Wendy Pitt, his personal assistant.

The U.S. representatives had not been informed by the White House of the defection, so they had no idea what Maceo was talking about and were unable to make any sensible reply.

Maceo walked out of the meeting, followed closely by the Russians as soon as they were able to get in their vitriolic speech denouncing American imperialism. By the time the conference had broken up, Maceo and the Cuban contingent were already on an Aeroflot flight back to Havana.

Immediately upon his arrival home, Maceo ordered ten hand-picked commandos, who formed his personal unit, to be ready to leave that evening. Then a staff car whisked him to the docks where he boarded what appeared to be a small fishing trawler, with the crew dressed as fisher-men. Actually, it was a government launch cap-able of outrunning any larger ship in the area.

Maceo changed into his "American" clothes, war-surplus fatigues. He looked the part of a slightly over-the-hill mercenary. He then settled into a bunk to await the rendezvous with *Wendy III*.

The Cuban military vessel reached the designat-ed spot before Senator Pitt's yacht. The captain cast anchor and waited, doubling the watch on the sophisticated radar screens. When radar reported the approach of a ship, the skipper still waited un-til identification was confirmed before going below himself to wake Maceo.

When Maceo arrived on deck, a small boat was lowered and the Cuban colonel was rowed over to *Wendy III*.

Senator Pitt offered his hand to help Maceo on-to his boat.

"Welcome aboard, Frank. Your information and help were invaluable. The American under-cover people got my daughter back in Vienna. She's probably in Washington by now. I came down here immediately. I figure I owed you at least that much."

The man Senator Pitt knew as Frank Mace, leader of a right-wing, paramilitary Cuban group dedicated to the overthrow of Castro, answered, "I am indeed honored that you chose to come here instead of waiting for your *hija* whom you have not seen for such a long time."

Pitt grinned and steered the man toward a chair on the aft deck. Then he took a seat himself, saying, "Perhaps a toast is in order. How about a rum?"

Before Maceo had time to answer, Pitt turned to the Cuban steward who stood at a table nearby. "Pour two short ones, Raoul."

When the steward placed the small glasses of white rum in front of the two men, Maceo said to him, "*¿Qué pasa, Raoul?* The rest of the crew, they are all on board?"

"*Sí, señor,*" Raoul replied.

"It's certainly an efficient crew," Pitt enthused. "I've nothing but praise for them."

Maceo's chubby face broke into a grin, not unlike that of a hungry barracuda. "They must go out again tonight. My troops will be ready for pickup."

"What do you mean? We agreed that my yacht was to be used only for picking you up. If I get caught running illegals the whole game is blown." Pitt's tanned face was a shade whiter.

Maceo shrugged. "This is the last time we need use your yacht. So we shall use it." Maceo lifted his glass and finished his drink in one gulp.

"I can't allow this, Frank. Someone followed me from the airport to the marina today."

"You are sure?"

"I could scarcely miss it, a yellow Ferrari. Whoever it is wants me to know they're watching."

"Who?" Maceo's high-pitched voice demanded.

"I think it's the Feds."

"Where were you waiting for your daughter when my message came to you?"

"I'm not at liberty to say."

"This person who followed you, we can take care of. Forget him."

"You can't do that! I know it's necessary to keep your presence in the States secret, but we don't want to kill people who may be on our side."

"This is a time of emergency, my friend. All our troops are to be mobilized immediately, because there are threats. We cannot risk this person spoiling it."

"What are you talking about? Your troops are meant to be mobilized to invade Cuba. What would they be doing inside the United States?"

"I assure you it is absolutely necessary."

There was a moment of strained silence as the two men stared at each other.

"I think you are mad," Pitt said.

"Do not worry, my friend. We shall not kill this government agent of yours. He can answer questions for us. I have men working at your marina, just as my men work for you on this boat. Now, tell me, where were you waiting for your daughter?"

"You don't expect me to betray my country?"

Maceo giggled. "I am here, my men are in your country. You have already betrayed it. To a traitor like yourself, what is one more little gesture?"

Pitt pushed his chair back and stood up. "I'm not going along with this."

Maceo didn't move. He just calmly waited. The steward came up behind the senator and slammed the sides of his hands down onto his shoulders, causing Pitt to collapse back into the chair.

"You shall not be allowed to leave until I am ready," Maceo told Pitt in a cheerful voice.

WHEN THE RUSSIAN TROOPS came bursting into the hangar, Bolan had a can of freshly mixed epoxy in one hand and a large brush in the other. There was no time to grab a weapon without being cut down by the sergeant and his four-man detachment.

Two guards were armed with Kalashnikovs and the other pair carried PPS43s. The two with the submachine guns did not point them directly at the man wearing the flight suit of an air force colonel. The barrels of the guns hovered just to one side of Bolan and Grimaldi.

The sergeant was a different matter. His uniform bore the maroon epaulets and piping of the MVD, the Soviet Union's Ministry of Internal Affairs, responsible for prisons and base security. His vz/52 automatic was trained on Bolan's gut. He knew the sergeant would not be averse to asking pointed questions, even of a colonel.

"What do you want?" Bolan demanded.

"A search of the entire base for a fugitive American pilot has been ordered, Comrade Colonel," the MVD sergeant replied.

"By all means, search," Bolan said.

Taken aback, the sergeant didn't move, and neither did the four guards. But their weapons still hovered as close to firing position as discretion would allow.

"You have seen no one?" the sergeant asked.

Bolan began to brush on the resin, working hurriedly so as to get the pocket formed before the glue began to set. As he worked he spoke in disjointed words, as if his mind was not on what he was saying.

"Sergeant, we must have this plane ready by tomorrow. We were too busy to notice if anyone came into the hangar."

The sergeant shrugged and indicated that his men should fan out and search the building.

Grimaldi and Bolan continued to prepare the Lloyd C-II for their escape while the sergeant and his unit carried out the search.

The soldiers were thorough. One paused by the Lloyd and watched Bolan's work with curiosity.

"That does not seem to be part of the original plane, comrade."

"Da," Bolan muttered. "All this for one special show."

The soldier wandered over to where Grimaldi was reassembling the fuel lines after a thorough inspection.

"May I look inside this plane, comrade?"

Bolan overheard the remark and thought of the missiles stashed in the rear of the aircraft. He raised his voice and spoke loudly enough for the sergeant to hear.

"You are friendly, comrade, but we are two nights without sleep. Please finish your search and leave us alone. It is our ranks, if this is not ready."

Bolan's words had their desired effect. The sergeant, jealous of his role as security chief, hurried to intercede. "The building seems deserted except for yourselves," the sergeant reported. "We shall leave immediately."

The sergeant motioned for his men to leave, then closed the door behind himself. Bolan walked over to a window and watched the five soldiers go. Only when he was sure they were in the clear did he nod to Grimaldi.

"Goddamn close. He'd sure like the glory of catching us himself," Grimaldi said. "The plane's ready except for two things."

Bolan raised an eyebrow.

"Fuel, and an unobserved place to take off."

Bolan walked to the door and switched off the light. Then he cautiously opened the door a crack. It would be dark in another two hours. His eyes searched the runway for a fuel truck.

The landing field was still heavily guarded, but Bolan could not tell if the perimeter was still sealed off.

"We're out of luck, Jack," Bolan told Grimaldi. "Why don't you check the other planes for gasoline?"

"It won't be enough," the Stony Man pilot said, beginning to sound worried.

Bolan noticed the look on his friend's face and

walked up to him. "What's really troubling you, Jack?"

"It's that sergeant. I've a feeling we're going to see him again. Somehow I don't think he swallowed our story."

"You may be right. He's MVD and he's suspicious. It doesn't leave us much time."

"We must have time! We haven't a chance to get this crate off before it's dark and the base settles down."

Again Bolan walked over to the door, opened it a fraction and peered outside. "Someone's approaching. I think it's the sergeant."

Bolan stood where he could not be seen immediately when the sergeant entered the building, and waited.

The NCO let himself in as quietly as he could and moved silently into the hangar. Bolan moved quietly in behind him before speaking.

"Comrade, you are both diligent and very suspicious. I like that."

The Russian whirled, drawing his vz/52. Bolan held up both hands to show they were empty. "Relax, comrade. You came alone this time. It is much easier to talk."

The man was plainly puzzled by Bolan's comments. "What are you talking about?"

"Your talents are wasted in the internal troops, my friend. I wish I had assistants as alert as yourself in the First Department."

"The First Department!" the sergeant breathed.

His puzzled expression told Bolan he was reaching the fine balance between curiosity and fear that would prevent the sergeant from regaining control of the conversation.

"Before I explain, please tell me what alerted you that I was not just another pilot making sure his plane was properly prepared? It could not be the uniform. Both my companion and I took great pains to be given regular air force issue."

"Part of the duties of the internal force here in Czechoslovakia is to guard transportation. These planes are considered museum pieces. No one would go about defacing them like that. I still see no reason for that thing you have attached to the aircraft."

Bolan smiled. "You must promise never to breathe a word of this to anyone else, comrade." When the sergeant nodded his head vigorously, Bolan went on, "Look on the floor of the rear cockpit."

The sergeant climbed up the side of the aircraft. He kept his automatic in his hand. When he caught sight of the missiles and launcher, his jaw fell open. He reached in with both hands and felt them to assure himself they were real.

Bolan could have easily drawn the silenced Beretta and finished the sergeant then, but that was not his plan.

"Comrade, how in the devil's name are you going to explain this?"

"There will be no need to explain," Bolan said in an icy voice, "but I like your style. If I should live through this, I would like you to consider transferring to my department."

The sergeant stepped down from the plane and moved around it to stand within two feet of Bolan, his gun hanging forgotten in his right hand.

"You may not be aware of this, comrade, but there has been an international conference on terrorism held in Vienna. It is breaking up early. Soon the fascist allies of the United States will be leaving that conference without making any commitment to lessen their bloodthirsty terrorism in Central America."

"I have heard of this conference."

"Well, comrade, two planeloads of lying imperialist lackeys are going to feel what terrorism is really about. This small plane will fly us low, under their radar, and they will not know what has hit them until one of those good Russian arrows flies up their tail."

"You will shoot down jets from that?" The sergeant gestured contemptuously at the Lloyd.

"An antiaircraft missile works as well launched from the air as from the ground. Only a small plane like this with almost no metal in its construction will get through the imperialists' radar. My friend and I have been given this glorious assignment, and if we return, I hope that you will come and work with me."

"But surely someone will find out?"

"You can search the files, my friend, but you will never find any record of this flight. And after tomorrow, there will be no record that this plane existed—that is unless we manage to bring it back. The chances are really not too unfavorable."

"A magnificent concept, comrade. I would have never believed it if I had not seen the missiles myself. It is indeed a brilliant stratagem. Is there something I can do?"

Bolan knew he had the man. "We could certainly use help, but we dare not use your duty time."

The sergeant laughed and said, "That is no problem. As of ten minutes ago my time is my own. I am not due on duty again until tomorrow afternoon."

"Very well, then," Bolan said. "First, tell me your name. For the future, you understand."

The sergeant, one Dimitri Trallug, was only too happy to comply as he smelled a transfer to the KGB.

"Something else you need, Comrade Colonel?" Trallug asked.

"Well, if you insist on helping us... Can you locate the gasoline truck? We cannot leave. We still have some work to finish here. The captain of the guard assured us that it would be within easy access of the main hangar door."

"I shall do it at once, Comrade Colonel."

Almost dancing in his excitement, the sergeant left the hangar. A chance to be part of a covert operation against the Americans and a possible future in the KGB were just too exciting to be contemplated.

As soon as he was gone, Grimaldi approached

the Lloyd, shaking his head. "Why did you let him go? He'll probably bring back half the base."

"He's MVD, but he wants to be KGB. That's why I'm so sure he'll come back alone. Let's push this plane to the door and wait for the truck."

Jack helped move the plane until it stood squarely in front of the folding hangar doors.

When that was done, Bolan told Grimaldi, "Now for your Russian lesson. *Da* is yes, *nyet* is no. Anytime I look at you and make any two movements, say *da*. If I make a single movement, say *nyet*. You got that?"

"One is *nyet*. Two is *da*. I suppose you think that will get me past this sergeant."

"It better."

It was an hour later and darkness had fallen when Sergeant Trallug slipped back into the hangar.

"I have been most successful, Colonel. There was a foul-up, but I have everything straightened out now."

Bolan glanced at the Russian coldly. "I hope you have not taken too much upon yourself, comrade."

The sergeant was taken aback and some of his affability slipped into nervousness. "I do not believe so, sir. The gasoline truck you needed, someone forgot to leave it in the proper place. It was not by the hangar door."

"And by now the whole camp knows I am here."

"No, comrade! I moved the truck myself. No

one is the wiser. I shall simply let the captain of the guard think that his orders were properly carried out.''

Bolan let out a loud, triumphant laugh. "I shall not forget this, Dimitri. You are an even more valuable man than I thought. I look forward to working with you in the future.''

The hours dragged by and the Russian sergeant kept watch while Grimaldi and Bolan performed needless adjustments on the engine to kill the time, and later brought in the hose from the tanker to fill the aircraft.

Bolan and Grimaldi wore all their excess clothing, knowing they would need every bit of it during the night flight in an open cockpit.

About 2:30 A.M. Bolan shook hands with Trallug. "We could not have managed without you, Sergeant. Now slip away so that you will have no questions to answer. You must remember that as far as this camp is concerned, this flight does not exist.''

The sergeant snapped a salute and disappeared quietly into the night.

Grimaldi took advantage of his dark blue mechanic's coveralls to follow Trallug through the darkness and recon the airfield. In ten minutes he was back to report to Bolan.

"The breeze is exactly right to go straight out this door, cutting across the runways, but we're about thirty feet short of take-off room to clear the far fence. There isn't enough light out there to see someone or any other obstacle on the runway.

And when we start this engine we're going to have every soldier on this base closing in on us. *And* it'll need a minute or two of warm-up time. I'm afraid this wasn't such a hot idea.''

"You can do it, Jack. I have one radio detonator and plenty of C-4 left. Perhaps it can provide us with both light and a distraction. Could you rev up the plane enough to take off straight ahead?"

"Yeah, but that would add rev-up time to one or two minutes' warm-up time. These babies aren't exactly quiet."

"You get ready," Bolan commanded. "I'll organize the distraction."

Then Mack Bolan disappeared into the blackness.

The overcast night and the strong, damp west wind were Bolan's allies as he stealthily moved toward the guards around the MiGs and Hinds.

The nightstalker circled them and came in past guards who stood hunched with their backs to the wind. Soon Bolan was crouched under the wing of a MiG with stamping and shuffling guards all around him.

Bolan stood up and hunched his back against the wind. He shuffled miserably toward the tank truck, past guards who paid him no attention. When he reached the side of the tanker, he quickly affixed the last of the C-4 and the last radio detonator. Then, bending into the wind, he shuffled away from the guards until he was out of sight.

Grimaldi was surprised to see him. "Back so soon?"

"We're set. Are the missiles loaded?"

Grimaldi nodded.

"Okay, Jack, show me how to turn this thing over and let's get going. Once the engine catches, I'll open the hangar door, then climb into the cockpit."

Jack showed Bolan how to turn the prop past the exhaust stroke onto the main compression stroke and then pull hard.

The pilot turned off the hangar lights, groped his way into the front cockpit, then pulled on his goggles. When Jack shouted, Bolan put his full weight into yanking on the five-foot wooden propeller. The engine caught the first time.

As Jack patiently coaxed the revving plane, Bolan folded back the hangar doors. The noise of the sputtering engine filled the night. Over the roar, Bolan could barely hear shouts. Some lights came on in buildings farther away.

Bolan put on his goggles, then carefully made his way to the rear cockpit. He slipped into the observer's seat, which faced the tail of the C-II.

The engine was at full roar and the plane was beginning to shake. Men had started to run toward the hangar. The Executioner could not hear them but could see them in the dim glow of the scattered lights that had come on.

"Time for a distraction," Bolan muttered to himself. He pressed the button on the radio activator.

The small plane shot out onto the runway just as a large geyser of flame erupted from the high-octane fuel truck.

A hundred feet out of the hangar, the wind was already whipping hard at the back of Bolan's head. He craned his neck to look forward over his shoulder. The chain-link fence was racing toward them and suddenly the plane was airborne. It dropped back to the tarmac, bounced once, then they seemed to spring up over it, clearing the fence by scant inches.

The Russian troops had still not recovered their wits sufficiently to fire at the plane.

Once clear of the army camp, the flight was tense but uneventful. Grimaldi held a southwest direction, keeping the plane within fifty feet of the treetops. In the darkness, he could not spot obstacles until he was almost on top of them.

They zigzagged down a path of blackness that they hoped would take them across Hungary and Yugoslavia, then across the top of the Adriatic Sea to their destination, Venice.

The only thing Bolan could do was huddle against the cold wind and marvel at Grimaldi's stamina.

Jack was always ready to fly any commission, anytime, no matter how dangerous. He exuded an intense concentration that excluded all else except himself, the flimsy airplane and the rushing land-scape.

There were no lights in the pilot's cockpit; Bo-lan did not know if it was equipped with lights or not. Either way, Grimaldi would have to fly with the instruments black in order to maximize his night vision.

Bolan estimated their speed to be between forty-five and fifty miles per hour. With their frequent changes in direction, the Russians would not find them before dawn.

They had only enough fuel to last until a bit past daybreak anyhow. It was ironic that they would have to land for fuel less than twenty minutes by jet from the army base.

Dawn found them outside the town of Polgardi, Hungary, not far from the tip of Lake Balaton.

And so did three MiG fighters.

10

Lao Ti stood between a mechanic's shed and a large diesel storage tank, watching the *Wendy III* being docked. The yacht quietly skipped into its mooring berth, a considerable contrast to the several power boats Lao had seen docked in the past few hours of waiting.

Two Cuban marina workers ran to take the yacht's mooring lines, something they hadn't done when other boats docked. From the deck, a short, corpulent Cuban barked questions in Spanish at the two workers. They paused from tying up the boat and pointed at Lao. This answer did not seem to satisfy the chubby man, who hurled out more questions. But the two men on the dock continued to point at Lao.

More orders were volleyed at the marina workers.

One of the Cubans answered, "*Sí*, Colonel Maceo."

The fat man was furious. Lao heard him repeat the name "Frank Mace" twice.

Contritely, the man said, "*Sí*, Mr. Mace."

Both dockhands turned and raced toward Lao.

Lao was interested only in what Senator Pitt

was up to. She had come for information, not battle. She was almost sure that the fat man who now seemed in command had not been on the *Wendy III* when it left the pier. He could have been below deck, but Lao thought it unlikely. It was more probable that Pitt was bringing in Cuban mercenaries. But why?

Lao stayed where she was, relaxed, watching as the approaching Cubans split and ran wide. They obviously expected her to start running. When she did not, they were plainly puzzled. They came to a perplexed halt six feet from her.

One of the men said, "Mr. Frank Mace, the gentleman on the yacht, wants to speak with you."

"I don't know any Frank Mace."

The two marina workers moved closer to Lao.

"We must insist," one said.

Both men lunged forward to take hold of Lao's arms. Lao pivoted and grabbed the arms of the two men, jerking downward. Stumbling, they landed on their faces in the dirt. Lao let go of neither wrist, but held the arms up away from their sides. Her small brougham shoes lifted one at a time and a toe cap smashed into each exposed armpit, hitting the nerve ganglia and rendering their arms useless.

Colonel Maceo shouted more orders, and more Cubans leaped from the yacht and raced toward Lao. But Lao did not attempt to run. She remained where she had been standing all along and watched as if all the action had nothing to do with her.

One of the charging Cubans produced a handgun, but Maceo barked an order and the thug hastily shoved it back into his waistband.

Maceo's screaming had brought curious marina members to the decks of their yachts to see what the ruckus was. Lao figured that if the Cubans started to use guns, they would be forced to massacre all the witnesses present. That they chose not to indicated to Lao that they had bigger plans.

The first of the attackers wanted the glory of getting Lao himself. From five feet away he launched himself into a body tackle. But Lao's body was no longer there. She seized his left arm and spun with his momentum, hurling him into one of his companions.

Then she grabbed another Cuban's arm and continued her spin, bringing the arm up in a hammerlock behind his shoulder, the wrist bent painfully backward. The man let out a howl of agony, which turned into a high-pitched scream as she put her other arm on his elbow and shoved, dislocating the shoulder and pushing him forward into one of the Cubans.

Colonel Maceo could not believe what he was witnessing. He knew his men would undoubtedly subdue the woman, but he could ill afford to have these men disabled.

He wanted every commando fit, ready to bring true terror to the United States. First, the main enemy—the group that sponsored Colonel Phoenix. They must go first, and then the rest of the American fascists would find out what terror really was.

The commander of the Dirección General de Inteligencia terrorists jumped off the yacht and ran along the dock as fast as his chubby form would allow. For all his excess weight, he was still in reasonable shape and had trained with his own elite troops.

Maceo had come within twenty feet of the mayhem when he saw one of his troops swinging a large wrench at the woman's head. She saw it, but too late and the tool impacted on her shoulder with crushing force.

Maceo heard the female warrior grunt as she sank to her knees.

There was a look of admiration in Maceo's eyes as he spoke to the wounded woman.

"Now you will come quietly with us," Maceo said.

Lao did not reply as she lay on the ground, grimacing and clutching her left shoulder.

Maceo snapped his fingers and two of his men picked up Lao and threw her roughly into the back seat of Pitt's limousine.

Pitt climbed in the front seat while Maceo and one of his lieutenants sat on either side of Lao. They left the marina quickly, before anyone could call the police.

"We shall take her to your place," Maceo told Pitt. "She has many questions to answer and I shall be delighted in forcing out those answers."

GRIMALDI HAD FLOWN SOUTH from Kosice, practically skimming vineyards to avoid enemy radar. The blast that had lit their takeoff had jarred the

MiGs and destroyed the helicopters. Neither Bolan nor Grimaldi doubted that the jet fighters would be after them with first light.

Over the border into Hungary, Grimaldi flew south of Budapest, then swung into an almost westerly direction as he headed on a course for Venice.

Huddling in the cockpit, Grimaldi looked at the fuel gauge. Their supply was critical. They would have to stop soon. If there was a chance to refuel the plane they had to be within four hundred miles of Venice to make sure they could reach it on the next tank of gasoline.

Bolan, sitting in the observer seat and facing the tail, squinted in the orange glow of the rising sun. The golden orb was just clearing the horizon when he spotted the three specks in the sky. He turned and tapped Grimaldi on the shoulder.

"Three planes on our tail. I think they're MiGs."

Grimaldi glanced quickly over his shoulder, then shouted above the noise of the engine and wind, "You're right. I guess this is where the fireworks start. They'll try to use their cannons. Launch the missiles when you think they're between one and two miles from us!"

Bolan leaned forward against the pull of his crossed safety harness and hand-over-hand took the launcher out of the pocket he had built for it. He placed the launcher between his feet, the tip sticking out of the cockpit, and repeated the process with one of the missiles.

He braced them sideways against the slipstream while he tried to fit the missile down the tube. By the time he had the job completed the MiGs were almost within distance.

Bolan knew he would get no chance to reload for a second shot. It would be strictly one missile for each pass by the jets.

The MiGs were closing rapidly but were several seconds from being within range. Mack Bolan spared a glance for the battlefield. It was magnificent.

Vineyards gave way to farm fields. There were large quantities of corn, interrupted by fields of cereals, ripe yellow, ready for harvest. An occasional field had already been cleared down to stubble.

Bolan listened to the whine of the fighters and as he concentrated on their approach, he had a fleeting impression of vultures swooping in on peace and beauty.

He tapped Grimaldi on the right shoulder and then raised the SA-7 launcher and put his eye to the sight. As the small plane veered to the right, Bolan exerted pressure on the trigger of the launcher until he could see a red light in the eyepiece. The control system was engaged. Bolan swung the scope to lock on the three fighters.

He could see they were fully armed, missiles hanging from the pods under the swept-back wings. He sighted on the MiG in the center, trying to put the cross hair on the intake jet next to the body of the plane.

One cannon started its rattle, and the bullets snapping past the light plane could be heard before the sound of the guns reached them.

Bolan steadied the launcher as best he could against the rushing wind, his aim never wavering from the air intake. Grimaldi kept the vintage aircraft dead on course.

Just when it seemed inevitable that the MiGs would either find their range or fly right through the flimsy C-II, a green light came on in the launcher's finder.

Bolan squeezed the trigger the rest of the way. There was a whoosh and the missile was on its way. A hundred yards out, the heavy booster charge ignited and the rocket quickly accelerated.

The MiGs had been coming in almost wing tip to wing tip in order to get the maximum field of cannon fire at the small plane. Now they scrambled to escape the missile their radar told them was coming their way.

With landing gear and air brakes still retracting, the throttles were pushed forward. The flanking fighters each broke formation, peeling off to either side.

To match the altitude of the Lloyd, the Russian pilots had been coming in very low. There was no room to dive. So the center MiG climbed, exposing its hot exhaust to the deadly heat-seeking head of the SA-7. Traveling at one and a half times the speed of sound, the phallic missile found and mated with the exhaust port of the fleeing MiG. The resulting orgasm of fire momentarily matched the red heat of the new sunrise.

The moment the missile left the launcher, Grimaldi threw the small plane into a climb, turning to get as much distance as possible toward their objective before the jets reached them again. Bolan, looking over the tail, saw the effect of his missile.

He also understood Grimaldi's battle strategy. He had managed to turn the plane and start climbing in a very short distance.

The two remaining MiGs were still picking up speed and for them to turn around meant making a huge circle, taking them to the limits of Bolan's vision. Traveling at full speed, they would have to fly larger circles to get a brief target alignment on the small plane.

As he thought this, Bolan struggled to load another missile. His forearms ached from the strain of keeping the missile and the cylinder lined up as he slid one into the other.

Grimaldi reached backward and touched Bolan. The Executioner slackened his harness and arched his back, leaning over the seat to put his ear next to Grimaldi's mouth.

"They'll try either rockets or strafing next. I'll use tight maneuvers. Fire as you can."

Bolan tapped Grimaldi's head twice to let him know the message was understood. Then the Executioner slid back into his seat and retightened his restraining belts. He would need both hands free to keep from losing the machine gun that he had in the cockpit with him, or losing the launcher and missiles from the open pocket.

The MiGs approached as Grimaldi had predicted, coming in almost level with them at four o'clock and eight o'clock.

Bolan lined up his launcher with the plane on his left. At its speed and distance he could not get a green locked-on mode.

In the scope he saw two missiles leap from the wings of the MiG. Bolan squeezed the trigger immediately. He knew Grimaldi would be taking evasive action.

Bolan barely had time to clamp the launcher between his legs—where the machine gun was stored—and slap one arm over the open end of the makeshift quiver. Grimaldi pulled the joystick back, taking the Lloyd into an inside loop.

Bolan expected the drum clips for the machine gun to fly out of the cockpit and perhaps hit him on the chin, but the centrifugal force of the loop kept the boxes on the floor of the plane.

At the top of the loop, Grimaldi changed into a roll and ended up flying straight between the approaching MiGs. The fighters turned in to hold their aim on Grimaldi as best they could. They were now at about nine o'clock and three o'clock.

Bolan's SA-7 missile had panicked the pilot of one plane into evasive maneuvers. At the same time, the other plane launched its two missiles. They missed the Lloyd, heading harmlessly for Lake Balaton.

As soon as the missiles whispered past the C-II, Grimaldi thrust the stick forward and executed a banked dive below the attacking plane. Even with

Grimaldi's drop, the Lloyd was severely buffeted by the backwash from the jet.

This time Grimaldi clung close to the ground, again speeding away from the battle scene.

Bolan, by twisting his head slightly, saw the wing come off the MiG he had fired at. His aim had been off but the pilot's evasive maneuvers had placed him in the path of a warhead from the other attacker.

Two down, one to go.

The last MiG pilot put his plane into a loop that would quickly bring him back for another strafing run at the C-II.

Bolan had no time to reload the launcher. He reached into the cockpit, picked up a 100-round belt-drum and snapped it into the Degtyaryov light machine gun. He then unfastened his safety harness and turned to kneel on his seat, aiming the machine gun at the jet as it came out of its loop.

Buffeted by the wind and cross breeze, Bolan considered the odds of a hit aimed at the air intake of a MiG approaching at two thousand miles an hour.

Screw the odds. He had to do it.

The jet came out of its loop, its machine gun yammering. Bolan saw two holes appear in one wing of the C-II.

The Executioner lined up on the fighter as best he could. When it seemed as if it was too late, Bolan pulled back on the trigger and held it down until the 100-round belt was empty. The MiG flashed by, tossing the small plane about violently.

A rip appeared in the wing fabric between the bullet holes.

The MiG completed its run and began to turn for another pass at the now-stricken Lloyd. Suddenly the engine started to cough and sputter, then died.

Grimaldi turned and yelled in Bolan's ear, "Turn around. Buckle up. We're going down!"

Bolan flipped himself in his seat, jammed the RPD between his legs, the barrel hot through the material of the flight suit. He slipped into the straps as Grimaldi put the plane into a speed dive, the engine silent.

Bolan craned his neck upward to watch the MiG prepare for the next pass. It hung suspended, as if on a thread. Then, suddenly, without power and almost standing on its tail, the MiG slipped sideways and began to spin. The canopy peeled back and Bolan saw the seat eject and a parachute burst out of it. It had been a low-level flight. He suspected the pilot stood little chance of surviving the parachute escape.

Grimaldi was circling, trying to find a field smooth enough to land the plane.

The fighter pilots in the MiGs would have reported the Lloyd's position. It would be touch and go whether they could get the plane down and find escape before the Russians arrived and spotted them, defenseless on the ground.

11

Carl Lyons pounded on the door of the Stony Man communications room.

"Go away!" Hal Brognola's voice called from inside.

"It's Lyons. I've got to talk to you."

The armed security guards at either end of the hall eyed Lyons uneasily. He was staff and they would not interfere, but they were tense, waiting for violence.

The electronic bolt clicked and the door opened. Lyons stepped inside.

"Shut it. I'm expecting another blast from the Oval Office any minute," Brognola growled.

Lyons kicked the door shut, triggered the bolt into place and looked around the room. It had become a shambles in the twenty-four hours since Grimaldi had been snatched.

The floor was littered with Styrofoam cups and mounds of soggy cigar butts, but there was no sign of smoke. A second glance told the blond warrior that pieces of cigar had been bitten off and spit out.

Before Lyons could speak, the telephone rang. Brognola pushed it through to the conference speaker.

"Yes, Mr. President," Brognola said resignedly.

The familiar voice of the U.S. chief executive filled the room. "Has Senator Pitt's daughter arrived yet?"

"Yes, Mr. President."

"And your missing pilot, is there any word?"

"Yes, sir," Brognola replied. "We have confirmation that his helicopter was attacked by two MiGs. When he tried to dodge beneath their missile attack he was taken out by a Hind. The same helicopter landed beside the wreckage and took our pilot with them. An eyewitness reported that the pilot was alive at that time."

"And Able Team did not go after him?"

"No, Mr. President. They felt it their duty to get Miss Pitt back to the United States for debriefing. They have now done that."

"But that pilot, Grimaldi is his name? Can he compromise us?"

"Yes, sir. But only under extreme pressure."

"Is Mr. Lyons at the Farm?"

"He's standing by. Go ahead, sir."

Lyons spoke up. "Yes, Mr. President?"

"Is Miss Pitt with her father?"

"No, sir. He left on business before we arrived." There was a moment's hesitation before the President asked the next question.

"What do you suggest that we do about our kidnapped pilot? It will be almost impossible to get an elimination team behind the iron curtain before he's forced to talk."

Lyons's voice grew frostier than usual. "I doubt that's necessary, sir."

"What do you mean?"

"A certain gentleman, for whom this operation was established, has agreed to rescue Jack."

Lyons was reluctant to mention Mack Bolan's name.

"You've been in contact with *him*! He's a wanted man. I need a full report on how he came to be on such a sensitive mission."

"There was some trouble at the pickup point. I have no idea how he came to be there, but he took care of it. When he saw that our transportation had not arrived, he agreed to look for Grimaldi. That's all I know."

"But he has no support apparatus."

"He had no support when he brought the Mafia to its knees."

The President ignored the gibe, snorting in derision. "You must have some idea why he was there."

"He heard of the defection from Russian sources. He was there to shoot Miss Pitt before she could defect."

"What?" That piece of news shook the President.

"He thinks that Miss Pitt is programmed to kill somebody here, probably her father."

"The man's mad! These are orders, Lyons. If Bolan comes within half a mile of Miss Pitt, I expect him dead."

Lyons's voice remained stone-cold. "Someone

may be mad, sir, but it's not Bolan. Able Team took the responsibility for Pitt. He'll do his job. I'll do mine. Is that satisfactory, sir?"

"No, but it will have to do. Is that new female operative of yours with Miss Pitt now?"

Hal Brognola took over the conversation. "Do you mean Lao Ti, sir?"

"That sounds like the one."

"No, sir. When the senator left in such a hurry, she followed him to make sure that he wasn't in trouble."

"If he finds out that someone's been following him, I may lose his support. Get that woman off his tail!"

"I can't, sir. We've lost touch."

There was a long silence, then the President spoke in a slow, measured tone.

"This is too much, Mr. Brognola. If you do not report to me within twenty-four hours that you have everything under control, I'll have no other choice but to send a CIA elimination team to find your pilot. And another to either arrest or eliminate this female agent."

"But, sir—" Lyons began.

"Twenty-four hours, Lyons," the President snarled and hung up.

"What next, Carl?" Brognola asked Lyons, who was already heading for the door.

Lyons snapped over his shoulder, "I'm not in Europe, but I'm going to find something to do rather than sit."

Brognola looked at the communications room.

He could not stray far from that if Stony Man was going to get things straightened out.

GRIMALDI HAD LITTLE GLIDING TIME in which to choose the best field for landing. He quickly selected one that had been cut to stubble. It was short, but there were no obstacles that could abort their touchdown.

The irony of the situation did not escape the Stony Man pilot. To escape being blown out of the sky by three sophisticated jet fighters, yet crash landing the wretched crate that took them out of Czechoslovakia.

The Stony Man flier banked once, coming in against the wind near a stone farmhouse at the end of the field. The only sound that could be heard as they swooped to earth was the air whispering past the guy wires between the wings and a slight whistle as it passed through the rip caused by MiG bullets. The countryside was equally quiet.

Grimaldi breathed a sigh of relief when he was close enough to the ground to see that farm machinery had been run in the same direction as ' is approach.

With the field rushing to meet them, he eased the nose forward, increasing their rate of descent, his eyes straining to judge the distance to touchdown.

At the last moment, he pulled the stick all the way back. His timing was perfect. The wheels brushed the top of the stubble, bounced once, then stuck in the soft soil. But there had been so little forward momentum left that the tail merely lifted and settled back down with the propeller intact.

"You need some practice with those landings, Jack," Bolan told the sweating Grimaldi.

The pilot managed a feeble grin. "Yeah, I know. Let's get this kite out of sight."

Bolan pointed to the small patch of grass that formed a lawn in front of the farmhouse. "How about over there? The trees along one side should make us difficult to spot from the air."

Grimaldi unbuckled his harness and jumped to the ground. Then he walked to one side of the plane and stood near the fuselage with hands on the lower wing close to the body. Bolan took the other side and they began to lift and shove the aircraft over the rough ground. It was difficult, slow work.

They had not pushed the C-II more than a couple of feet when a voice spoke from beside the house. Bolan didn't understand the language, but figured it was Hungarian.

He responded in Russian as he moved away from the plane and saw an elderly man standing at the front door of the farmhouse.

He spoke again, this time in an accented but distinct English. "Your Russian is atrocious, but your accent is decidedly American. My comment was to the effect that your toy airplane will not fit inside my house."

Bolan had no time to debate a plan of action. He decided to act on instinct. He'd trust the farmer; it was quicker than playing games.

"I thought we'd be less visible from the air if we parked on your front lawn."

"Perhaps. But you'd be in plain view from the road. May I suggest you use my implement shed instead? I think your aircraft would fit there."

Bolan and Grimaldi approached the man. The farmer was small and his age was hard to determine. He had a neatly trimmed white beard that contrasted starkly with his weather-darkened skin. He was wearing overalls and a faded blue shirt.

As he pointed to a long, low shed set well back from the farmhouse, it struck Bolan as odd that his hand appeared never to have seen a day's manual labor.

"It is too great a distance to push even that light plane by yourselves," the farmer told them. "I shall bring my tractor."

He was gone before either Bolan or Grimaldi could reply. The two warriors waited, listening. An engine behind the house coughed and backfired, finally settling down to a grumbling roar.

Soon the farmer was back with an ancient, battered tractor that looked as if it had gone through the front lines of World War II.

As the farmer hooked a tow rope to the single landing wheel under the tail, he explained, "When the mechanics at the state collective can no longer keep their tractors running, we peasants with independent farms are allowed to buy them."

He towed the Lloyd into the implement shed, out of sight from both the air and the road. Then he ran the tractor over the stubble field until there was no trace of the landing. Only when that was done and the tractor had been put away once more were Bolan and Grimaldi invited into the farm-house.

Two-thirds of the ground floor was taken up with one large room that served as kitchen, dining room and family room.

Standing at an old-fashioned, wood-burning stove with her back to them was a young woman. Long, braided blond hair swung freely down her back to below her shoulder blades. She wore trousers of some rough homespun fabric and a cotton blouse. Her feet were laced into sturdy work boots. She finished turning eggs in a huge iron skillet then turned and examined the two strangers with interest.

Bolan immediately found himself attracted to this woman with rosy cheeks, flushed even more by the heat from the stove.

"It is time, I think, for introductions. But it might be better if we used first names only," the farmer said. "My name is Janos and this is my daughter Mariska. She speaks only Hungarian, I'm afraid."

Bolan returned the introductions, then thrust his hand out to the farmer.

The farmer had a firm grasp. But again Bolan found it strange that the delicate hand belied the weather-beaten countenance.

The daughter said something in Hungarian and then stepped forward with her hand out. As she shook hands with each man, she carefully pro-nounced his name. The direct gaze of her blue eyes and her open manner appealed to Bolan more than all the flirting and coquetry in the world.

The ritual of meeting over, she turned to her father and they exchanged a rapid dialogue in Hungarian.

Janos interpreted for their visitors. "Mariska says that she has put on extra sausages and eggs for you. Will you join us for breakfast?"

"Thank you," Bolan answered.

As Bolan and Grimaldi washed up for the meal, Grimaldi asked, "How far are we going to trust these two?"

"As far as we have to. They may help us, they may betray us, but the odds of getting back into the air with their help are better than trying it alone."

"Uh-huh. But I'd sure feel better if I knew about Janos's English. It's too good for a Hungarian farmer."

"Judging by his hands, he hasn't been a farmer very long. Let's play it by ear and see what happens."

Jack nodded as he dried his face on a coarse towel.

Bolan and Grimaldi were wolfing down the simple breakfast when they looked up to see Janos and his daughter studying them.

Slightly embarrassed, Grimaldi said, "We haven't eaten since—"

"Please, no explanation is necessary." Janos cut him off by raising his palm.

After the meal, Mariska gathered the empty dishes, placed them in the sink and went outside.

Janos opened the conversation by getting straight to the point.

"Well, gentlemen, now comes the awkward moment. You are here in a plane that's either out of commission or out of gasoline and you've not asked me to contact any authorities. My English is much too polished for a small farmer in a Warsaw Pact country. And there is the problem of how much information to reveal. Have I summed up the situation correctly?"

Bolan nodded, forcing Janos to continue.

"My story is quite simple, really. I am Hungarian by birth. But I taught agricultural economics at Harvard for twenty years. My wife died in childbirth before I left for the United States. I felt that my daughter would have a better life with my childless sister-in-law and her husband. They agreed to care for Mariska during my absence. But when my wife's sister passed away last year, I decided to return home.

"It took me very little time to apply my economics and management skills to farming on my return to Hungary. I found that I liked it. Soon I was running the collective to which my daughter and I had been sent. So now you know my story. I hope that I have given you a chance to decide how much you wish to tell me."

Before Bolan could reply, Mariska returned with a tall, intense young man. His brown eyes sparkled as he took in the strangers. He and Mariska sat to one side, waiting for Bolan to speak.

"The truth is simple," Bolan said. "My pilot friend, Jack, was shot down over Austria, forced into a Russian helicopter and flown to Kosice. I went after him and we managed to escape in the museum piece you have in your shed.

"We had to shoot down three MiGs to get this far. So I guess the Russians are anxious to have us back. We need a place to hide until dark, ordinary gasoline for the plane and a place to take off."

The young man spoke for the first time, addressing Janos.

"Three MiGs were shot down just north of here this morning. I think he speaks the truth. In the cockpit of the old plane there is a launcher, two missiles and a Russian machine gun."

The young man turned to Bolan. "Around here they account for every liter of gasoline. If Janos or other farmers give you gasoline, the secret police will know where it went."

"So you can't help us," Bolan said.

The young man's mouth broke into a smile that didn't reach his eyes.

"I did not say that. If you want gasoline, you must take it from the Russians. You can buy help with your missiles and launcher."

Bolan considered the young Hungarian for a few moments.

"Before making a decision, I must have the whole story."

It was the young man's turn to study Bolan during a long silence.

Finally he said, "My answer means your life. If I tell you details and you are captured, many will die, slowly. If it looks like capture, we shall have to kill you ourselves."

"I already know Mariska brought you here. You'd have to try to kill us if we went on our own at this point anyway."

"It is easier to deal with a man who knows the truth. You are right. The same applies to members of our own cell. Four have been captured and are to be driven to Moscow today. We plan to stop the convoy. If we can rescue our friends, we shall. If not, your rockets will assure the safety of others."

Bolan nodded. His heart went out to these brave people—nearly forty years under Soviet domination and yet their wills were still not broken.

He said, "Let's hope for a rescue. Our plane can still use those SA-7s for defense."

The young man shook his head. "No, the price of our help is the rockets. Even if we succeed this time, there will be other times."

"How do we get our gasoline from this?"

"The convoy will consist of five vehicles. They have large tanks because they have much distance to go. They will be freshly fueled. If you can stop the trucks with your machine gun, we shall supply the patriots to wage war without burning the trucks." The young man stopped and grinned. "Besides, there will be fuel and spare parts left over for us."

Bolan nodded. "When?"

12

Within the hour, Bolan, Grimaldi, Mariska and the young man, whose name was Agoston, were joined by four other partisans. They set out immediately for the rolling foothills where the convoy would be compelled to slow down in order to negotiate a narrow cut in the rock face.

Bolan carried the RPD light machine gun. Grimaldi lugged the spare drums of ammunition. Mariska was armed with the only handgun in the group, a pre-World War II Hungarian automatic.

Most of the rest of the group carried captured Kalashnikovs. Agoston and one of his lieutenants carried the SA-7s and launcher.

Bolan, Grimaldi and the Hungarian freedom fighters split up into two groups and positioned themselves on the rock on either side of the gap, above the road.

Their objective was to take out anyone in the truck cabs and allow the vehicles to come to a stop as best they could. The guerrillas were sure of the route, but had no idea when the convoy was due in the area.

They settled down for a´long wait. Mariska lay

next to Bolan at the far end of the cut away from the vehicles' point of entry.

The warrior cast an appraising glance at the woman, wondering whether the handgun was meant for the enemy or for himself, in case things should go wrong.

The wait seemed interminable, broken only by Mariska's occasional movements as she tried to make herself comfortable; each time she was closer to Bolan.

After a while they lay side by side, touching the length of their bodies. Distracting, yeah, but a touch of humanity and warmth in this hostile environment.

The sound of the trucks laboring up the incline reached their ears before the convoy appeared. Bolan finally saw five Zils with canvas canopies behind. Before he could warn Agoston, the rebel leader opened fire. The battle was committed and Bolan could do nothing but join in.

It was a brief firefight. The guerrillas at the entrance to the rock cleft took out the drivers and guards of the last two Zils. The two freedom fighters across the road from Bolan riddled the occupants of the two front vehicles.

They swerved into the walls of the embankment and came to a halt. The driver in the middle truck had no choice but to slam on the brakes as both the road ahead and its retreat were blocked by driverless vehicles.

The first soldiers who jumped to the ground were cut down by automatic-rifle fire.

One of the Hungarians called out in Russian for the troops to surrender.

Bolan was alarmed by the absence of Gaz 4x4 gun trucks and by how few soldiers were actually in the vehicles. He sprinted toward Agoston. The rest of the guerrillas had moved among the trucks to rescue their friends and disarm the few Soviet soldiers who had surrendered.

Even before he reached Agoston's position, Bolan heard Hind gunships. For a transport carrying rebel prisoners, there had been too few guards. The Executioner saw the trap even as the jaws of the air defense were snapping closed.

Bolan found the young Hungarian frantically shouting to his men.

"We must pull back," Agoston said.

"We're dead if we do," Bolan told him. "Can you get your men to follow my instructions?"

"You have a plan?"

"Yes."

"What would you like us to do?"

A shout went up from the rest of the rebels when their companions emerged unhurt from one of the trucks.

Bolan quickly issued instructions to Agoston as the prowling choppers closed in.

"Chase the Russian troops up the road. Tell your companions to stand in the middle of the road with their hands above their heads. They must surrender to the helicopters. Get the rest of your men out of sight and give me that missile launcher and the missiles."

"It is suicide."

"We have no choice."

Agoston shook his head and shouted down into the cut, first in Hungarian and then in Russian. The Soviet troops did not need a second invitation to get out of range of the approaching gunships.

One of the Hungarian prisoners began to argue. Agoston cut him off with three short words. Then the two Hinds were there, a menacing presence above the scene of ambush.

The Hinds darted back and forth over the cut. The Russians were trying to evaluate the situation, but the pilots were having difficulty making the seven-ton helicopters hover.

Plainly, whoever was in command was puzzled. The only people in sight were their Hungarian prisoners with their hands in the air and a few Russian soldiers still running up the road.

As Bolan had figured, the commander decided that the prisoners were still worth taking alive, perhaps to answer questions. One gunship continued to claw at the air, frantically trying to hover above the scene, while the other descended two hundred yards away to disgorge its troops.

Grimaldi caught up to Bolan at the peak of the hill, and they both raced toward the landing helicopter. Agoston was hard put to keep up with them. Bolan was carrying the launcher armed with one missile, and Agoston the second missile. Grimaldi had the light machine gun and two drums of ammunition. It made an awkward load.

"When I get in position, cut down those

troops,'' Bolan ordered. He stopped running and hoisted the SA-7 launcher to his shoulder, aiming it at the exhaust port of the airborne Hind. He squeezed the trigger until the red light came on. The green light flashed on immediately and Bolan finished the trigger pull.

The helicopter slued sideways and crashed twenty feet from the cut, the blast knocking some of the enemy troops to the ground.

Grimaldi opened fire with the RPD machine gun. The eight troops who had disgorged from the Hind fell like wheat under a scythe. Bolan and Agoston hastily loaded the second air-to-ground missile. Then Bolan sprinted toward the sitting helicopter.

The chopper was already taking off. Grimaldi's bullets were ineffective against the heavy armor and reinforced glass. At one hundred yards out, Bolan stopped and trained the SA-7 launcher on the rising Hind.

The gunner tried to swing his Gatling gun on Bolan, but the Executioner was too far to one side. The gunship crew reconsidered their situation and the pilot touched down again.

At a gesture from Grimaldi, they moved their hands off the controls. The pilot opened the door and stepped down. After a moment's frustration, the gunner broke open his top hatch in the nose of the chopper and climbed out also.

Bolan indicated the crew members. "Keep those guys under guard. Ground troops will be arriving any minute. You and your men see about transporting the fuel. Jack and I will slow down the Russians.''

The young rebel leader motioned to the Hind. "You mean that you will turn the monster on its masters? But why do you not use it to escape?''

"These machines drink fuel. They can't fly more than a hundred miles without refueling," Grimaldi broke in.

"Then I suggest we destroy the machine after disabling the Soviet ground troops. The Russians have less than a hundred of those things. Each time they lose one, they scream in pain.''

Bolan nodded and raised an eyebrow to Grimaldi, who said, "Let's go.''

The Stony Man pilot climbed aboard the Hind and started checking out the instrument panel. Bolan lowered himself into the gunner hatch underneath Grimaldi, then picked up the helmet with the intercom mike. He fitted the helmet, then stared at the array of buttons and switches on the firing-control panel.

He tried the intercom. "Jack, I'll need your help.''

Grimaldi's voice was clear in the helmet. "Hold it till I get myself oriented. I studied everything in the Stony Man computers on these babies until I went cross-eyed, but it isn't the same as sitting here.''

While Grimaldi busily acquainted himself with the controls and dials, Bolan watched the activity in front of him.

The Hungarians had split up into two work

crews: one group drained gasoline tanks while the other rounded up weapons and took spare parts off vehicles.

The spoils of battle were quickly loaded onto an old farm truck, which two more rebels had driven from a side road after the battle was over. Bales of hay had been tossed off the truck and would be piled again on top of the gasoline and weapons.

After a few moments, Grimaldi spoke again. "I'm ready. How are you doing?"

"The Gatling gun's okay, but how do I fire the pods on the wings?"

"Pull the sighting mechanism down from your right and fit it comfortably in front of your eyes," Grimaldi directed, pausing only long enough for Bolan to carry out the instructions.

The pilot's seat was situated above Bolan in the nose of the Hind, so Grimaldi could not see what Bolan was doing.

"Now, the joystick between your legs is the aiming mechanism. The four toggle switches on your right arm the pods. We seem to have unguided air-to-ground missiles. When you flip the switch, a green light will come on when the pod is locked into your control mechanism. Then you aim and press the firing stud on top of the joystick."

"Got it," Bolan said. The props on the Hind frantically beat the air and the heavy machine lurched toward the sky.

Grimaldi followed the road, flying about one hundred feet up, watching for a convoy of ground troops. They found it only three miles from the ambush site.

Five Gaz 69s with mounted machine guns and two more Zils full of troops sped along the highway to close in on the rebels.

Bolan flipped the first toggle switch. The ready light came on immediately. Bolan's left hand guided the joystick with which he aimed the pod of thirty-two deadly missiles, while his right hand hovered over the next switch.

When the sights lined up on the convoy the first salvo caught the first two trucks and the next two piled into them. The middle trucks were hit before they could brake and the last salvo took out the last two Gaz 69s.

The only truck that had not been hit piled into the flaming wreckage ahead of it. The Hind clawed awkwardly into the air and began a long sweeping turn back to the spot where they had left Agoston and the Hungarian rebels.

The moment the Hind landed, Agoston issued some curt instructions to a couple of his guerrillas. Two men ran toward a bale of hay, picked it up and scattered it around and inside the aircraft. Agoston threw a match into the scattered hay as they began their trek back to the World War I airplane.

They were half a mile away when they heard the explosion. They stopped and looked back. The flames were already shooting a hundred feet into the air.

"One demon down," Agoston muttered. Then

he thrust out his hand to Grimaldi. "We cannot thank you enough for what you did."

It was a five-mile hike back to Janos's farm. The former lecturer helped Bolan and Grimaldi patch the wing of the Lloyd.

Just after midnight, Janos towed the refueled antique plane to the two-lane country road. Rebels were posted to prevent any oncoming traffic. Mariska and Agoston thanked the Americans for helping rescue their friends from the Soviets.

The flight across Yugoslavia was as tense as the one the night before. Hedgehopping through the dark, Grimaldi could not see obstacles until he was almost upon them.

The first crack of dawn found them skimming the white sand beaches just south of Trieste. Once out over the Adriatic, they turned north toward Venice.

The sun was rising when Grimaldi brought the small plane down at the airport at Lido. They had no radio, but the airport was not yet busy and they managed to get in without being demolished by a private jet. For the first time Bolan was happy that his seat did not face forward in the plane.

It took less than a minute from touchdown for the Italian police to have two cruisers bracketing the small plane.

HAL BROGNOLA WAS STARING in disgust at the telephone in the Stony Man communications room. His usually impeccable gray suit looked as if it had been slept in. Actually, Brognola had not had it off for forty-eight hours. The same time had covered his cheeks with a gray stubble and his eyes were bloodshot.

When the telephone finally rang, he snatched it up and demanded, "Who's on this line?"

The abruptness startled the Italian NATO operator who stumbled twice before regaining the use of her English. She had a call, Priority 23, for Mr. Brognola or senior officer present.

Brognola dropped the handset in his frenzy to reroute the call through the proper scrambler. After he had punched the right buttons, he fished the handset from the litter of old coffee cups and broken cigars.

"Brognola here," he barked.

Jack's voice had a slightly tinny sound. "It's a beautiful morning, Hal."

"Jack! What's the status?"

Jack's voice became guarded. "I'm at the airport at Lido. Seems the airport security office has a CIA scrambler. Strange. But they're not asking me questions about my passenger, who's still sitting in a 1916 airplane out on the runway. So I'm not asking about the scrambler."

"He's with you, then?"

"Yeah."

"You fit to fly?"

"I could use two or three hours' sleep, but I'm fine. What did you have in mind?"

Brognola paused for a moment, frowning. The CIA were looking for Bolan. Certainly, they had to get Bolan at least to the States. He could take care of himself from there. But not to the Washington area! Both Able Team and the President were too damn nervous about that Pitt woman. He needed an excuse to land Bolan elsewhere.

"Jack, things are still hot for the big guy around here. I want to persuade him to help us out in Florida."

"You know damn well he'll do it. What's up?"

"Pitt left for Florida before he saw his daughter. Lao Ti flew down to the New Tamiami Airport to keep an eye on him. Now Ti isn't reporting in. Ask Striker to find Lao for me."

"Isn't that something you could handle better from there?"

"Not really. The Company was supposed to leave her a car there. She picked that up. I want to know if the Company is up to something. Striker can move without official circles knowing a thing. Sell it to him."

"Got it. Give us something fast to make it convincing."

"Hold on."

Brognola punched Hold and put through an inside call to Kurtzman in the computer room. Although it was about 1:00 A.M., Kurtzman was monitoring his various nets, searching for word of Grimaldi. He answered the internal telephone on the first ring.

Before Kurtzman could say anything, Brognola snapped, "Bear, get on your net. Find the fastest way to bring Grimaldi and an unspecified passenger back from Italy, near Venice."

"Right," Kurtzman said.

Brognola waited nearly a minute while Kurtzman rode the computer nets and soared through the military data banks. Then he was back on the line.

"Hal, the Italians have some F-15C Eagles that are due to be flown back to Missouri to have their radar updated. You could probably arrange to have one delivered to Grimaldi immediately. You'd also have to arrange a midair refueling."

"You make the arrangements. Let me know who I have to okay it with afterward. Just do it fast."

Brognola hung up without waiting for Kurtzman's reply and put Grimaldi back on the line. "Jack, snatch a couple of hours sleep. I'll get busy and clear you with the Italians. An Eagle two-seater should be there within a few hours. I'll arrange for midair refueling on your way to Florida."

"Great, Hal! Even with the detour to Florida I should see you in about seven hours. Or should I stay around and help with Lao?"

"No, we need you here. Try to keep the identity of your passenger secure, especially from the Company. It might not hurt if something happened to the scrambler you're using. Maintain radio silence. Of course, break off the radio bit when necessary, as in the midair refueling and the landing. Got all that?"

"Loud and clear, Hal. 'Nobody's' going to Florida and I'll be up there as soon as possible. In the meantime, silence is the key word. Hang loose."

The line went dead. Brognola hung up the phone, left the room and strode down the hall to relay to Able Team the news of Grimaldi and Bolan's safety.

Unable to find Able Team in any of the recreation areas, he simply stood in the middle of the hall and hollered until the Officer of the Day came running.

"Where the hell's Able Team?" Brognola demanded.

"An Air Force chopper picked them up about eight hours ago, sir. They said they're taking Miss Pitt to Florida to see the senator and to find out what happened to Miss Lao."

"What kind of helicopter?"

"I saw them leave from our helipad, sir. It was a Sikorsky S-76."

"They'll be there by now. Damn!"

Just then the PA system paged Brognola to the computer room. Brognola took off running.

When Brognola pushed into the computer room, Aaron Kurtzman waved a telephone receiver at him.

"The duty officer at the Pentagon wants your okay. All the arrangements are made, including the midair refueling. But you have to assure him that you have the authority."

Assuring a green duty officer that he had the authority was not that easy. He finally convinced the DO that it would be more diplomatic to wake his superior for confirmation than to wake the President. It was an hour and a half before everything was straightened out.

Brognola raced back to the communications room and let himself in. "Get me the scrambled line at the security office at Lido airport," Brognola instructed the officer.

Twenty minutes later the officer returned. "I'm sorry, sir, but it seems that Mr. Grimaldi sabotaged the scrambler equipment before he left. The Eagle arrived within forty minutes of when you were speaking to him. He's already on his way here."

13

It was 2:00 A.M. when the hearse and limousine from the Shady Pastures Funeral Home pulled up to the main gate of the Homestead Air Force Base.

Fred Zansky, owner of the funeral home, climbed out of the limousine. Irritated, he motioned his son, Fred Jr., to stay behind the wheel of the hearse. Two in the morning was a hell of a time to pick up a stiff, but Fred had served in World War II and his son in Vietnam, and if a serviceman needed them at this hour, they would be there.

Zansky tugged at the jacket of his gray suit to get rid of the creases, then fingered the knot of his maroon tie before stepping up to the guardhouse at the entrance to the base.

"I'm Fred Zansky and that is my son, Junior." The undertaker turned and pointed to the hearse. "I'm looking for someone named Lyons."

The blond man who stepped forward was about six foot two.

"I'm Lyons. What's your rate per day?"

"Ah, it. . .it depends on how many miles are to be traveled. Where is the body to be taken?"

"There is no body, yet. We just need some inconspicuous transportation."

Zansky looked at his pearl-gray limousine and matching hearse, both with extra double chrome. "Inconspicuous?" he blurted.

"This is Florida. People come here to die. Hearses are more common than taxis."

"Well, there are a good number of funeral homes, I'll admit, but surely. . ."

"How much?" Lyons interrupted.

Zansky wanted no further part of this cold-eyed menace. "For both vehicles with drivers, one thousand dollars until 3:00 P.M. We're booked for another funeral at four."

Lyons reached into his pocket and produced a roll of hundred-dollar bills. He counted out ten and slapped them into Zansky's hand.

Then Lyons turned and spoke to a group in the shadows of the guardhouse. "Load up. We've got wheels."

Two men and a woman with long, blond hair opened the back of the hearse and began to pile in baggage. At this point, Fred Jr. bounced out of the hearse.

"What's with the ammunition boxes and attaché cases for MAC-10s?" the ex-Green Beret asked.

The big blond man turned to look at him with eyes that could have frozen a candle flame. "Shut up," was all he said.

Fred Jr. gulped. "Yes, sir." He climbed back into the hearse.

Lyons nodded to Gadgets. "You ride with Junior. We'll follow and keep an eye on you."

Gadgets stepped into the passenger seat in the hearse. Lyons sat in the limousine beside Zansky, and Blancanales and Wendy Pitt got into the back. Wendy still carried an attaché case containing the M-11 she had chosen from the Stony Man armory.

As they pulled away from the air force base, Gadgets gave the younger Zansky a downtown address. They rode in silence until Fred Jr. worked up the nerve to ask, "What's this place we're headed for with enough weapons to start a revolution?"

"A CIA safehouse."

"You guys CIA?"

"Hardly."

The safehouse turned out to be an old warehouse just off Flagler Street. Able Team held a quick conference on the sidewalk.

"Gadgets, you stay and watch our drivers and Miss Pitt. Pol and I will go in. If his diplomacy fails, mine will succeed," Lyons said, patting the Colt Python under his left armpit.

Blancanales squeezed the woman's hand. "You stay here," he said.

She raised the attaché case. "Will I need this?"

Blancanales shook his head. "No, this is just a friendly call," he said and followed Lyons to the door of the import-export company.

Lyons pounded on the wooden door several times without results. He raised a combat boot and sent it smashing through one of the door panels. He reached inside, unfastened the catch and went in.

Blancanales drew a Beretta 93-R and cast a

quick glance on their backtrack as they entered. They hadn't moved down the hall more than ten feet when doors opened on either side of them and they found themselves covered by two men with Uzis.

"Just hold it right there," a tall blond man said.

Lyons and the CIA agent faced each other.

"You Williams?" Lyons asked.

"Who wants to know?"

"A friend of Lao's. She's missing."

"I don't know what you're talking about."

Lyons shrugged. Ignoring the guns pointed at him from both sides, he turned and walked farther down the hall. Blancanales had no choice but to follow. The two operatives moved out of their doorways and covered the Able duo from behind.

"Freeze," Williams commanded.

From the open door came Gadgets's voice. "No, you freeze. I won't miss two head shots at this range."

The agents realized they'd been suckered into the hallway. They turned to find a silenced 93-R trained on them.

Williams and his sidekick did not have to decide what to do. Surprise had made them momentarily forget Lyons and Blancanales. Numbing blows on their forearms caused them to drop their Uzis. Lyons kicked the guns down the hall out of the way.

"Time to talk," Lyons said.

The CIA agent who had not spoken to this point, asked, "What do you want?"

"The radio gear to trail the homing device that you put on the car you gave Lao."

"What homing device?" Williams asked.

Politician sighed, then said, "We don't have time for games. The Company wouldn't lend a vehicle to a rival agency without making sure they could find it when needed. Now, we're asking your help to locate it."

"Or?"

"Or we simply tie you and leave you here. I'll phone the newspapers first. I'm sure you'll enjoy telling all those reporters what the CIA is doing with an operation inside the United States."

Williams rolled his eyes. "Okay. You win, for now. The radio gear's in my office."

"Get it," Lyons told him.

With the small tracer supplied by the CIA, Able Team did not locate the yellow Ferrari until 4:30 A.M. Gadgets got out of the car and double-checked. There was no question—it was the car with the CIA beeper.

Blancanales and Wendy Pitt climbed out of the limousine and opened the back of the hearse. Pol rummaged around in their gear until he found his *jo*, a white oak stick about as big around as his thumb and four feet long. When he had his fighting stick, he and Wendy joined Gadgets by the car.

"A yellow Ferrari?" Pol exclaimed.

"Trust the CIA," Gadgets said.

Lyons was not paying attention. He was scanning the area.

"We have company," he told his companions.

Cubans armed with knives and clubs were closing in on them. They were moving quietly but were completely unconcerned about whether they were seen or not.

FERNANDEZ MACEO KNEW how to extract information from people. Had he not been the best pupil of General Abovian? But in this case Maceo had no time to employ the mind-numbing techniques that were certain to produce information from Lao Ti. It could wait until later. In the meantime, the woman would be locked up and kept under strict surveillance.

Pitt's house had not been designed to detain captives, but the hurricane cellar proved an adequate holding cell. There were no windows, and the sturdy door was easily barred. By Maceo's orders, Lao was thrown into the bare room and the door locked. She was left drinking water, but no food.

The orders to the guards were strict: check on her periodically, keep her water fresh.

As Maceo busied himself getting his undercover army mobilized, Lao was neglected, except for a periodic check by a guard. While Maceo arranged the defenses of the Pitt household, Lao sat cross-legged in the center of the cement floor and meditated.

Maceo's plan was simple. Around the house on Key Biscayne he placed only those guards who would attract no undue attention. The main body of his men collected in Crandon Park, posing as tourists and campers.

Many of the men quietly took over yachts in the private marina. Each pair of men had a CB radio. Any attack on the house would bring the men pouring south along the only road, sealing the area and slowly enclosing the house and eliminating the attackers.

Maceo was content that his plan was perfect. More men arrived hourly. By the time his elite troop arrived on the *Wendy III*, he would be ready to begin his reign of terror.

As the hours passed, the guard's curiosity grew.

The woman sat so still that often he had to look twice to make sure she was still alive.

The guard prepared for yet another inspection of the prisoner. He removed the barricade from the door to the storm cellar. Next, he drew his Ruger Super Blackhawk from his belt holster.

The .44 revolver felt good in his hand. Its weight assured him that he held a good bludgeon should the prisoner try anything. He held the gun tight against his hip where it could not be grabbed or kicked.

This time the woman was not sitting in the lotus position. She had fallen backward and lay on the floor. Her right leg was bent with the knee up. It had to be a trick, the guard thought.

Still, he approached cautiously. Then a smug look crossed his features. He nodded as he figured out the ruse. The woman would hook her left leg behind his ankle while the right one would snap forward, striking him in the knee and breaking it. It was a standard prone fighting maneuver, and he would not fall for it.

He looked again, there was still no sign of breathing. She could not have held her breath that long. If something had really happened to her, Colonel Maceo would have his head. The guard decided that he must investigate immediately. If the woman was dead, he was in trouble. If she was faking, he would teach her a lesson.

He was mere inches from the woman's prone form when he felt a touch on his ankle. He started to swing the heavy Ruger.

Instead of flashing toward his kneecap, the cocked leg swung to the side, causing the prisoner to roll over onto the knee with her buttocks in the air. The revolver swung harmlessly over the top of her leg, which had never risen far enough to hit the guard's knee.

The foot that had brushed his ankle shot upward like a piston. The sentry's movement had caused him to bend toward his intended victim. The heel of the foot smashed his right temple, sending skull fragments into the brain.

Lao Ti checked to make sure the guard was dead, then picked up the belt holster and gun. The belt was much too large for Lao's small waist, so she slung it over one shoulder and across her breasts. The long gun hung down under her right arm where it would be least in the way. She strode out of the storm cellar into the predawn darkness, determined to find Andrew Pitt.

There was fifty feet of open lawn between the storm cellar and the back door to the house. A lone sentry carrying a Dragunov guarded the rear entrance.

The sentry looked up and saw a small figure gliding across the lawn toward him. He brought up his weapon, but in the dim light the person kept approaching. Now he could tell it was a woman wearing something over her shoulder, but it was only when she was within three feet that the sentry recognized his fellow guard's weapon.

The lookout started to squeeze the Dragunov's trigger, but he was too late. Before the trigger finger could finish its travel, the woman's leg flashed up, the heel crushing the man's voice box. He dropped, quietly choking on a throatful of mashed larynx.

There was a light in the kitchen window near the back door. Lao guessed that those Cubans still awake were congregating there. She glided to a shrub at the corner of the house and peered around. Another guard patrolled the side of the house. Lao melted into the shrubbery and waited.

Half an hour later, someone discovered the bodies and raised an alarm.

Guards raced from either side of the house to see what was wrong. Lao slipped out of the shrubbery to the unguarded side of the house and let herself in through an unlocked window. She stood still and listened.

The house was silent. Light streamed in from the kitchen and Lao recognized the dining room.

Any guards who had been in the kitchen had dashed outside when the bodies were discovered. She moved silently to another doorway that accessed a hall. Lao paused there for a moment.

A flight of stairs led down into the hall. It appeared as if all the guards had rushed outside. Lao retraced her steps and peered around the doorway to the kitchen. It was still empty.

Lao returned to the stairway and stealthily climbed to the second floor.

She gained the landing there and paused, checking the layout. The doorways into the upstairs hall were arranged in facing pairs. Only one door did not face another across the hall.

Lao moved silently to the door and tried it. It was not locked. She pushed it farther in and slipped inside the room.

It was the master bedroom. From the moonlight streaming through the window Lao could see a double bed, and against one wall was an entire row of closets.

On the surface of a dresser that stood next to the bed was spread the mishmash of a man's pockets. On the other side of the room, where there would normally be a woman's dressing table, were an easy chair, a floor lamp and a bookcase.

The owner of the room sat in the easy chair, apparently unconcerned about the commotion in his yard. As she entered, Lao could see the thatch of white hair turn toward her.

"No light," Lao ordered in a soft voice.

"I recognize that voice. You're the Oriental from Stony Man, the one who was taken prisoner at the marina." Pitt kept his voice low so it would not carry outside the room, but he did not whisper.

"Correct," Lao told him. She glided across the room and sat on the bed facing him.

He leaned forward and squinted at her. "And you've escaped from Maceo."

"Yes. He threw me into that hole in your backyard."

"I knew his real name wasn't Frank Mace. I didn't really care what it was as long as I had a right-wing officer capable of getting back at the Cubans for kidnapping my daughter."

"Right wing? You do not know the name Fernandez Maceo?"

"Should I?"

"I learned of him during my indoctrination at Stony Man. His specialty is psychological conditioning. He is a colonel in the Cuban secret police. His responsibility is the terrorist arm of the DGI. The woman who calls herself Wendy Pitt was his chief assistant."

"Then the Cubans have had me a second time." Pitt's voice was bitter with self-condemnation. "We were over there to help the Cubans. I was young then and it was the in thing for left-wingers to go through Canada to Cuba and help with the sugar harvest, to try to undo some of the damage done by the U.S. embargo. We were thanked by having our three-year-old daughter kidnapped.

"That's when I decided I would do anything and everything to help with the downfall of the Castro regime.

"I pretended to be sympathetic to Cuba. I figured no one would ever suspect. And now I find that I have imported an army, not dedicated to the overthrow of Cuba, but to the overthrow of my own country. I'm a traitor."

Lao studied the man in the easy chair. The pieces of the puzzle were beginning to fall into place and she wanted to get as complete a picture as possible to take back to Stony Man.

"Why did you leave Stony Man before seeing your daughter?"

"You brought me that message that Maceo was on his way. I believed he was being smuggled in and out of the country and that once he was committed to the trip, could not go back. I considered it essential to his life that I meet him whenever I got a message." Pitt ended with a short self-derogatory laugh.

"A pity you didn't get to see your daughter. Would you be able to tell if she was an impostor or not?"

"If she's the same one Maceo showed me a photograph of, there's no doubt she's my daughter."

"Is there a telephone here?"

"I had one, but Maceo had it taken from my room. No one says I'm a prisoner in my own house, but I am. He's been using the telephone all night. The receiver is in my study, downstairs."

"Maybe we can—"

Lao was interrupted by the sound of the door opening. She dropped quietly to the floor with the bed between her and the door, but she wasn't quick enough.

The Cuban entering the room saw a blur of movement. He ran toward the bed, tracking his M-16 on the spot where he'd seen the movement. As he leaned over the bed, a hand grabbed his ankle from underneath and pulled. He fell backward heavily and two hands twisted his foot, forcing him to roll onto his stomach. Suddenly a human dynamo rolled from under the bed and managed to get to her feet in the same time it took the guard to get to his knees.

He swept the assault rifle up with his right hand, his finger inside the trigger guard. Before he could bring the M-16 to bear, one small, incredibly strong hand seized his wrist and another slammed into his knuckles, bending the hand toward the arm, forcing the fingers to open. The gun fell to the floor.

The terrorist swung his left fist into the ribs of the small woman in front of him. She rolled with the punch but was forced to release the cramped hand. The Cuban did not try to regain his feet, but launched himself in a head-first dive at his assailant.

Two small cupped hands came together over his ears with tremendous force. There was a huge explosion of pain inside his head as eardrums ruptured. He sank back down, forgetting the fight.

He never saw the single knuckle blow that cracked his temple.

Senator Pitt opened his mouth to say something, but shut it again when they heard the sound of running feet approaching the bedroom.

14

Carl Lyons calmly counted the Cubans moving in on Able Team. Six of them, carrying clubs, knives and chains. Apparently they were no more anxious than Able Team to have shots shatter the predawn quiet of the city.

"Can you use that toy you're carrying?" Lyons asked Wendy Pitt.

Blancanales and Lyons looked at Pitt. Her body was tense and she was biting her lip.

Pitt's voice had a slight quiver in it when she said, "I recognize several of those men. They are DGI."

The men of Able Team wondered what members of the Cuban secret police were doing in the United States, but they did not waste precious seconds on questions that could be asked later.

"Can you use the M-11?" Lyons insisted.

The woman took a deep breath and nodded.

"Then protect the vehicles and drivers, but don't shoot unless attacked."

"*Sí,*" Wendy Pitt said.

Lyons told Pol and Gadgets, "No guns unless they start. Keep one alive." From the tone of his voice he might have been planning a quiet picnic.

Able Team spread across the narrow road, close to the yellow Ferrari that Lao had abandoned. The approaching Cubans broke like a wave and moved to surround the three cars and six people.

Pitt extracted the M-11 from its attaché case and slammed in a 32-round magazine. The DGI terrorists took no notice and continued to surround the group. The loudest sound on the key was the shuffling of booted feet and the occasional clink from chains that two of the terrorists carried.

Lyons continued to issue calm orders. "You work clockwise, Pol. Gadgets and I will go the other way."

Carl Lyons fired a front snap kick to the testicles of a terrorist who had carelessly come within range of Carl's long legs. The man went down, howling in agony.

A man whirling a bicycle chain attacked Blancanales, the weapon slicing the air like a buzz saw. Pol lunged under the deadly chain. His *jo* made a sweeping arc, breaking his attacker's ankle.

A knife wielder lunged at Gadgets. The thrust came low and never stayed still long enough for Gadgets to get in a kick. The Cuban knew how to handle knives, but he was completely unprepared to meet a master in the business.

Gadgets blocked the maneuver to move the knife arm out from between himself and his opponent. The blademan spun out of the way and danced right into the path of Gadgets's own knife, which slid in under the ribs with surgical precision, piercing the terrorist's lung.

Gadgets heard movement behind him and spun in time to see a goon with a club charging at full speed, intent on knocking Gadgets's head into the ocean.

The electronics specialist seized the elbow and wrist of the club arm and continued the twisting motion with the momentum of the club until the arm was dislocated at the shoulder. As the terrorist lost his balance and fell backward from the wrench on his shoulder, Gadgets sank to one knee. His opponent dropped over Gadgets's other knee, helped by an arm on the chest and the legs. The spine snapped.

Another DGI terrorist with a knife closed in on Blancanales, while the terrorist with the broken ankle was pawing for hardware beneath his shirt. Pol drove his heel into the sternum of the prone fighter, sending bone splinters into the heart.

Blancanales retrieved his *jo* and lunged toward the rushing knifeman. The *jo* slammed to one side, its tip crushing the attacker's nose and driving him back.

The man with the smashed nose recovered his equilibrium and with a roar he charged at Blancanales. Pol parried the knife thrust and spun one end of the stick, cracking the guy's skull.

Lyons ran to catch up with the last terrorist, who was farthest from the action. The Cuban had seen his comrades were no match for the crazed *gringos*, and dropped his knife and ran, trying to grab the automatic under his shirt. Lyons quickly overtook the terrorist.

A sudden forward snap of Lyons's karate-hardened fist made jelly of the terrorist's vertebrae. The man fell and the gun hand, still wrapped around a Browning Hi-Power, was turned to mush under Lyons's boot. Lyons finished him off with a kick to the head.

Blancanales had taken one bloody-faced prisoner alive. Gadgets dragged by the collar the DGI goon whose testicles had been introduced to Lyons's boot. He still seemed too immersed in his own pain to answer questions.

Able Team turned their attention to the Cuban with the smashed nose and battered eye. Blancanales shot question after question at the DGI terrorist, but he responded to none of them.

Lyons stopped in front of the prisoner and glared at him, but the prisoner would not raise his eyes. Ironman's hand snaked out and grabbed the man by the hair, lifting him until his toes barely touched the ground. The eyes flashed open and words flowed from a suddenly loosened tongue, but before the terrorist could put together a comprehensible sentence, he fainted.

Able Team's attention was drawn to the other prisoner.

Wendy Pitt had walked over to where he was lying on the ground. She leaned over him and shot a long speech at him in rapid Spanish. Politician watched, perplexed, then a hard smile slowly turned up the corners of his lips.

The suffering man mumbled two or three words. Pitt clubbed him with the M-11 and the

Cuban, still doubled over with both hands clasped between his legs, let out four quick, choppy sentences.

Pitt nodded once, brought the M-11 up and put a single bullet between his eyes. She then swung the weapon and emptied the last few bullets into the other prisoner.

Wendy Pitt went back to the limousine, removed the empty clip and replaced it with a full one.

"What the hell did you do that for?" Gadgets demanded.

"We no longer needed them," Pitt answered casually.

Lyons knew no Spanish. Gadgets's grasp of the language was slow; Politician was the only one who had followed what had gone on.

"How did she persuade him to talk?" Gadgets asked.

"She merely told him that we'd send him back to Cuba and reminded him of what the options were," Politician explained. "Either he'd be shot—Castro had the Cuban troops who survived Grenada shot—or he'd be sent to Angola with the regular army."

"What about Lao?" Lyons asked.

"She was taken away in Senator Pitt's car," Blancanales said.

15

At the sound of running footfalls down the hall, Lao Ti silently vanished into a closet.

Two DGI terrorists toting M-16s burst into the room.

"No está aquí," grated one.

They moved toward Pitt and almost tripped over the body Lao had left in the middle of the room.

The Cuban who had not spoken whipped his assault rifle up toward the senator. The sights never lined up on their mark. A small fist smashed into the gunner's kidneys. The Cuban gasped, dropped his rifle and fell to his knees.

His companion swung around, momentarily taken aback by the sight of the woman coming at him. With blurring speed, Lao's hand crashed into his carotid artery. The Cuban's eyes rolled upward as he fell lifeless to the floor.

Lao snatched the M-16 and threw it to the senator. Then she picked up the assault rifle her first victim had dropped. He was still on his knees, his face ashen as he struggled to overcome the waves of pain that threatened to engulf him.

The senator watched in horror as the woman

slammed the weapon's butt alongside the Cuban's head, knocking him unconscious.

"What do we do now?" Pitt asked Lao.

"Somebody will be following up by now. That's the advantage of being part of a team. The problem is to remain alive until they find us."

Lao walked to the window and looked out through the pane. Pitt was alerted by the intensity of her gaze and followed her, peering over her shoulder at the front of his large estate.

From her vantage point, Lao saw that the property appeared to be surrounded by a thick cedar hedge, about six feet high.

The driveway started to her right, but the actual entrance was screened by a sauna/change-room building and another length of the hedge that shielded it from the road. The driveway curved across the front of the property and approached the house on Lao's left. It then continued its arc to parallel the front door. Then it widened and curved around the house to the back.

In the middle of the property was a round swimming pool surrounded by a tropical garden, which in turn was bracketed on three sides by the driveway.

As they watched, two five-ton trucks appeared at the gate. Cubans materialized from hedges and undergrowth and from inside the house, moving with the caution and assurance of trained soldiers. The covered trucks rolled past the house, stopping near the corner. By straining to look at an extreme angle to the right, Pitt and Lao could watch the

Cuban terrorists unload wooden crates and metal containers.

"There's enough arms there to replay World War II," Pitt exclaimed.

Lao said nothing, but started to smash out the windowpane. Before she could shoot, Senator Pitt's limousine powered around the corner of the house and skidded to a stop next to the trucks.

From the back seat, Maceo pointed out the car window at the falling glass. Lao and Pitt only had time to throw themselves flat before a hail of gunfire took out the rest of the window and half the frame.

"That arms delivery is probably what Maceo was waiting for. He does not have to stay undercover anymore. You watch the door. I must try to destroy those munitions," Lao said.

The senator nodded and scuttled over to the doorway. He lay flat on the floor and opened the door to give himself a line of fire into the hall.

Lao stood up again and approached the window, trying to remain out of sight. She knew the chances were not good. If gunfire did not get her, they had merely to torch the house.

Lao managed to edge up to the window without being shot at. The air seemed especially still and quiet after the barrage of automatic-weapon fire. Maceo's high voice carried clearly as he issued orders from inside the limousine.

"There are some upstairs. Send enough men to kill them. Blast through walls if you have to. If the noise of guns brings outsiders, I have more than one hundred men waiting to block the Keys and take care of the trouble. I must leave now to meet my lieutenants on the senator's boat.''

As the limousine screamed around the curved drive, Lao tried to edge closer to the window, but another hail of bullets drove her back. She knew that while she was being pinned, the weapons and munitions were being unloaded.

As ABLE TEAM, the two Zanskys and Wendy Pitt left the marina, a woman who had been sitting on the flying bridge of a sport-fishing boat watching the brief battle, pulled out a small two-way radio.

She spoke urgently into the mike, ''Rolling Eagle, this is Betsy Ross.''

''Rolling Eagle here. Come in Betsy.''

''The pride have left. They're in a gray hearse and gray limousine, pulling out of A-1 Marina now. Have Big Indian follow and send Rolling Home for me.''

''Rolling Home coming for you. Big Indian will follow hearse and limousine. Ten four,'' the radio crackled back.

Lilith Fernley dropped the small transceiver into her handbag, clambered down a ladder and jumped onto the dock. Then she marched down the wharf toward the road.

Five minutes later a forty-foot-long motor home flying a small American flag and sprouting a dozen types of antenna pulled to a stop in front of her.

She stepped aboard and spoke to the driver. ''Send Williams and Spider to see me.''

The motor home was under way as she walked through the dining area to a private room at the back. Two men entered the room as she lit a cigarette.

"Our hounds just showed up at the marina. I don't know how they did it, but they're on their way to Pitt's. You two take your sniping positions over the estate and when he shows up, *don't miss.*"

"How do you know he'll show up?" Williams asked.

"Don't ask stupid questions. He showed up in that park in Austria to pull their nuts out of the fire. I know he'll show up again. And you two better be ready to take him out."

"Those three are tough. And they *are* on the same side," Williams said.

"You are tiresome," the woman screamed. "Why can't you be like Spider? He knows enough just to point and shoot. You'd better learn that, too. No one's on the same side as the Company. Now, what are your vantage points over the senator's grounds?"

"We have blinds high in two laurel oaks beside the estate. Everything is in range from either location."

"Good. Don't fail," the woman said.

The motor home stopped near the Pitt estate. Williams and Spider set off across neighboring lots to reach their sniping posts just outside the Pitt property. Each carried a Springfield M1A rifle equipped with a 10-power scope, and extra magazines of mercury-filled bullets.

"I don't like letting those guys get wasted," Williams confessed. "They're just three guys trying to do the same job we are."

Spider gave Williams a disdainful look. "They point 'em out, you shoot 'em. You stay alive longer that way."

"So you've got orders to hit this Colonel Phoenix, or whoever he is, when he shows up. But why are we letting those others walk into a trap?"

Spider shrugged. "And what does the Company do when those guys find out we brought in the Cubans?"

"Hell! You're Cuban. There's a lot of right-wing Cubans around."

"They're all DGI. Take my word for it," Spider spat. "That Frank Mace had us fooled like he fooled Pitt."

"Why didn't you say something to Lilith?"

"Hell! She knows. We'll take care of them eventually, but if Washington finds out that we brought terrorists into the country, we are in one heap of trouble."

"I don't like letting those guys die just because we had another screw up."

"Lilith says do it, we do it." Spider's voice didn't sound particularly happy, but it did ring with determination.

"How come we do everything Lilith says?"

Spider, a veteran of over fifty CIA assassinations, looked up at his big, blond compatriot and made a confession of his own. "That woman scares the hell out of me."

CARL LYONS HAD COLLECTED Pitt's address before leaving Stony Man. When he gave it to Fred Zansky, the funeral-home director said, "Hell, that's only five minutes from here."

Able Team was still on Crandon Boulevard when Gadgets ordered Fred Jr. to stop the hearse. The sun was just fighting its way over the horizon and there were no other cars in sight. The sound that had prompted Gadgets to stop the vehicle came again—a short burst of automatic-weapon fire.

The Able Team members scrambled to the back of the hearse to prepare for a shooting war. Lyons strapped on the Python shoulder rig over his flak jacket, then quickly fastened a web belt that held grenades and extra ammo for the Atchisson and the Python. He snatched up the Atchisson and slammed home a 7-round box magazine. Each shell held a mixture of both number two and double-ought steel balls.

Gadgets took time to remove the silencer from his 93-R and return it to the shoulder rig under his shirt. He grabbed a loaded Ingram SMG holding a 30-round magazine of .45 ACPs. Spare clips, a communicator and some fine tools were in the web belt the electronics specialist wore.

Politician slipped his *jo* into his waistband. Instead of a web belt, he threw on crisscross bandoliers, then picked up the M-16/M-203 combination assault rifle and grenade launcher.

Wendy said nothing. She checked that her MAC-11 was loaded and stood silently by.

The two Zanskys looked at each other nervously. "We'll take you guys there, but we ain't staying around to have these cars shot up," Zansky Sr. told them.

No one answered him. He stared at the three battle-hard faces for a few seconds, then silently got into the limousine.

As they neared the gates to the Pitt estate, a limousine shot out and narrowly missed the lead hearse. Gadgets had a quick glimpse of a round swarthy man in the back seat.

"That wasn't the senator. Keep going," he told Fred Jr.

The property appeared quiet as they wheeled through the gates and proceeded up the curving sweep of the driveway. Junior was the first to see the terrorists closing in behind them and jammed on the brakes.

"Behind us!" he shouted.

His speech was punctuated by a burst of fire from an M-16. Able Team and Wendy Pitt didn't wait to hear any more. They rolled out of the vehicles before they came to a stop.

The Zanskys found themselves alone in the middle of a blazing firestorm. Both men tried to shove accelerator pedals through floorboards. The limo and hearse leaped forward past the surprised terrorists who were firing at the house and unloading the supply trucks. Before they could react, both Caddys were out of sight around the back of the house.

The two vehicles almost balanced on their noses when the Zanskys discovered there was no rear exit from the grounds. The elder Zansky ran from the car and heaved open garage doors of the four-car garage. Two slots were empty. Father and son quickly backed in their cars and slammed all the garage doors shut.

As he pushed the last door down, Fred Jr. asked, "What do we do now?"

"Hide. This isn't our fight."

"But there're only four of them, including the woman. There must be a hundred Cubans running around with guns out there. How come we're hiding in here and letting them take on a foreign army?"

Fred Sr. put an arm around his son. "We paid our dues as soldiers, son. Good soldiers with records to be proud of. But we're not heroes. If we look after ourselves, we're doing more than most people. I guess we just gotta leave the tough ones for the heroes."

WENDY PITT CAME OUT OF her roll and regained her feet. Automatic-weapon fire burst over her head and she squatted, bringing up the MAC-11, looking around for enemy targets.

All she could see was Cubans, the same Cubans she'd trained and been trained with, the same Cubans she'd dispatched on terrorist missions throughout the world.

Another burst of bullets dug up the lawn beside her. She jerked the gun around but was unable to bring herself to fire. She was frozen.

A hand grasped her fist, practically dragging

her across the driveway. With automatic-weapon fire snapping over their heads, Blancanales pulled the woman through some shrubbery toward the swimming pool. They came to a small hollow around a sundial. Pol pushed her out of the line of fire and continued to move on by himself.

The next moment, all three Able Team warriors pushed their faces into the flower beds as death sent thousands of lead fingers streaking over their heads. Pol lobbed two frag grenades toward the trucks but was unable to raise himself high enough for accurate aim. The grenades fell short, taking out only two terrorists.

Suddenly two explosions tore up shrubbery close by, covering Able Team with dirt. "They've moved RPGs down the driveway and straight south from the trucks," Gadgets reported. "They have us on three sides."

"Pull back," Lyons commanded.

Pol reported from his position closest to the gate. "We can't. There're troops swarming in through the gates. More than a hundred of them."

16

Bolan remained in the Lloyd C-II while Grimaldi made arrangements to get them from Italy back to the States. The few mechanics who came over to the plane paid no attention to the American.

Ten minutes later a car came for Bolan and he was transported to a private hangar where he was given the use of the office and washroom.

Shortly, Grimaldi heaved his way into the office, dragging two duffel bags.

"Taxi's waiting," he said, handing one of the sacks to Bolan.

"What's this?" he asked Grimaldi.

"I managed to get us some goodies in a swap for the plane," the pilot replied as he stowed the bags with difficulty in the F-15C Eagle trainer.

The two Americans lifted off within an hour of landing in the Lloyd. This time they clawed their way to the top of the world and screamed westward at nearly three times the speed of sound.

Bolan closed his eyes as his mind turned to the Hungarian rebels. They were just like him, in a way, fighting for justice and freedom. Especially freedom. He hoped that what he and Grimaldi did to help the guerrillas would not land them in further trouble with the Russian masters.

The sound of Grimaldi's voice in the helmet earphones intruded on Bolan's thoughts.

"I have the umbilical in sight now," Grimaldi was saying.

Bolan stared through the clear plastic bubble over Grimaldi's shoulder. He could see the tail jet and two wing jets of a McDonnell-Douglas KC-10. The huge tanker dragged a hose, the end of which was a bell-like cup. Grimaldi was concentrating on slipping the nose of the Eagle into the bell.

A coupling that Bolan had not seen before slowly extended from the nose of the Eagle at five hundred miles per hour as Grimaldi maneuvered the needle into the bell. Bolan said nothing, respecting the pilot's intense concentration.

The coupling was made and the fuel started to flow, occasionally releasing a spray of fine mist if the air turbulence affected the fuel line too much.

As the Eagle gained weight from the fuel, Grimaldi had to slowly increase his pressure on the throttle to keep the connection.

When the refueling was completed, Grimaldi informed the tanker and held his position until the flow was cut off. The Eagle retracted its feeding tongue while the tanker extended the gap between the two planes. Then Grimaldi slowly shoved the throttle forward and the Eagle screamed its way higher into the sky at a 45-degree angle, the ground-speed indicator steadily moving up the dial.

"Congratulations," Bolan muttered into his helmet speaker before drifting back to sleep.

Bolan came awake as Grimaldi was getting his landing instructions from Homestead Air Force Base in Miami.

"You awake, Mack?" Jack asked.

"Yes," came the crisp reply.

"Then it's time for a quick briefing. I promised Hal you'd do him a favor. You're Jack Grimaldi. I'm an Italian pilot. By the time we get the mess straightened up in Washington, you'll be long gone.

"The bags contain play toys for you. An army colonel with an interest in Pietro Beretta just happens to be an old-plane nut. We made a very good trade.

"Brognola has rented transportation waiting. It'll come right up to the plane and you're cleared for special delivery of these two emergency packages."

"What's the favor, Jack?"

Jack hesitated. It might have been to make a course correction, but Bolan had the feeling Grimaldi was reluctant to go into the next phase.

"There's a new member in the Stony Man group, Mack...."

Bolan sensed the delicate area that was giving Grimaldi problems. "A replacement for April?"

"In the computer field, and sometimes in the battlefield. She's an extra body. No one could be a replacement."

Grimaldi switched over to the radio to acknowledge his landing-approach instructions. The conversation was not continued until the plane was on the ground and taxiing to a corner of the field. They were once again out of touch with the tower.

"The new lady's name is Lao Ti. She disappeared while tailing Senator Pitt. Another agency has been keeping a tight eye on Stony Man, and Brognola doesn't want to send out anyone they know about. He'd like you to find out what happened to Ti."

"This serious?"

"Yeah. Some agency's making a power play. We've got more trouble from our side than from the other side."

"What can you tell me?"

"Only the senator's address."

He gave it to Bolan and popped the canopy as a Mercury Cougar raced across the landing strip toward them. "This'll be your wheels."

"Thanks, Jack," Bolan said, reaching forward and giving Grimaldi's shoulder a squeeze.

Bolan dislodged the two bags from the cramped compartment of the Eagle and turned away from the aircraft.

Grimaldi started down the runway before the car arrived.

The driver of the car was a young brunette wearing an Air Force uniform. She popped the trunk open from inside the car and Bolan stowed the two bags. He then climbed in beside her.

"My instructions are to take you to the gate and

turn the car over to you, Mr. Grimaldi. Is there anything else I can do?''

Bolan was still wearing the peasant clothing supplied by the Hungarian rebels and his own blacksuit underneath. If the driver of the car thought his clothing was strange, she did not comment on it.

"Just keep me moving," Bolan told her.

A few moments later she pulled the car to a stop by the guard gate. She watched as Bolan drove away.

The brunette went into the guardhouse, picked up the telephone and dialed a number.

"He just left the base," she reported.

"Grimaldi?" a female voice asked.

"No. It's *him*."

"That's fine. We have snipers waiting for him," said the voice, and hung up.

From the gate of Homestead Air Force Base, Bolan took the nearest entry to the 821 turnpike. He pulled off at the service plaza and drove to a remote corner.

In the early-morning light there were a few trucks and one or two cars in the plaza.

First, he checked his route on the map provided in the glove compartment of the rental car. Once he had his route memorized, he opened the trunk and checked his gifts from Grimaldi.

The first bag contained two cases of 9mm parabellums, spare clips for the 93-R and for the Heckler & Koch MP-5K submachine gun, both of which still rode under his farmer's clothing. There were also a dozen defensive frag grenades, the latest NATO technology.

Bolan decided the two weapons would be sufficient, so he left the second bag stored in the trunk.

It took a while and it was awkward, but Bolan managed to load the 93-R and MP-5K, slipping extra clips into the blacksuit without quite undressing in the parking lot.

Bolan did not hit the first roadblock until he had crossed the Rickenbacker Causeway, past the entrance to Crandon Park. Four swarthy men who could have been Hispanics flagged him down. They were wearing combat fatigues and each carried an M-16. They had an assortment of handguns in hip holsters and one carried a two-way radio.

"The road she is closed up ahead, for an hour," one of them told Bolan. The voice was heavily flavored with Spanish.

With the car stopped and the window open, Bolan could hear bursts of automatic-weapon fire.

"I have an important message for United States Senator Pitt. I must go through," Bolan said.

The response was not what he expected. All four started to swing up their M-16s. The Executioner jammed the shift lever into reverse and floored the gas pedal. The Cougar left black tracks as it spun back along the road.

Bolan slid down in the front seat, using the outside rearview mirror to keep the car on the road. Two rows of small holes appeared across the top of the windshield as the car rounded a curve and sped out of sight.

Bolan put some distance between himself and the roadblock, then stopped off the road. He removed the overalls and stripped down to the black fighting suit.

He knocked out the bullet-scarred windshield with the butt of the MP-5K, then powered down the passenger window. He started the car and flicked the lever to Drive, keeping his foot on the brake. He pushed the snout of the MP-5K through the front windshield's frame, which acted as a gun mount for the weapon. He had a clear field of fire.

With his left hand gripping the wheel, he tromped on the gas pedal, the powerful car eating up the distance to the roadblock.

The Executioner began firing the moment the four Cubans stepped onto the road. They hardly had time to bring up their M-16s at the rushing Cougar. Bolan slowly swiveled the SMG as he drove past, the 9mm parabellums chewing up vital organs of the Cubans as they collapsed lifelessly to the ground.

Bolan's vehicle hurtled south toward the end of Key Biscayne. The sounds of battle grew nearer. He was not totally convinced that Senator Pitt's estate had become a battleground, but considered the odds favorable that Able Team was involved.

As he crested a slight rise, Bolan took in a sight that made his jaw drop. He brought the car to a halt and jumped out to stand on the hood for a better view.

A large estate with a curved driveway was the scene of a pitched battle. Men in combat fatigues were pouring in the front gate. And there appeared to be more than a hundred of them. The dense hedges funneled them back toward the center of the frontage.

Withering fire from a few automatic weapons in a garden in the center of the grounds was holding the troops back. They were having difficulty getting onto the grounds, and the open space made it difficult to close in on the garden. But the numbers were overwhelming, and from grim experience Bolan guessed the defenders stood little chance of survival.

Two fire teams armed with grenade launchers were spreading out from some trucks close to the house, setting up to aim the launchers into the garden area.

Suddenly, as Bolan watched, first one, then a second member of a fire crew dropped. The bullets could not have come from inside the garden area.

It took Bolan only seconds to spot the sniper just outside the estate in a tall oak. It took his victims no longer to spot the source of their misery. Shouting their rage, those not yet inside the gate detoured toward the tree.

Bolan did not wait to see more. He jumped off the hood and slid behind the wheel. The Executioner picked up the still warm MP-5K and slammed a fresh clip home.

As the car swung forward, Bolan guided it with

his left hand while his right index finger caressed the trigger of the SMG.

The Executioner picked the hindmost of the charging troops, giving himself the longest possible time before the enemy realized they were under attack from the rear.

Over the noise of battle he heard the distinct booming that could only have been Lyons's Atchisson.

17

Carl Lyons did a lightning assessment of the situation. The odds did not favor Able Team. It would not be long before the grenade launchers chewed up the entire garden area. That left one choice—go through the small group defending the supply trucks.

"Move out!" Lyons shouted.

Then he was on his feet, leading the way, running through the flower beds. Single shots from the Atchisson announced his coming and hundreds of fingers of death reached out ahead of him, groping for terrorists.

Gadgets and Blancanales followed Lyons's play without question. Pol scooped a hand under Wendy's arm, jerked her to her feet and propelled her along with him.

Gadgets's MAC-10 sprayed one flank while Pol's M-16/M-203 hybrid hosed the other.

Almost a solid wall of lead poured at their backs from the entrance to the estate, but the shooting was wild and sporadic, and suddenly it seemed to die in great shouts of confusion.

On the second floor of the large house, Pitt told

Lao Ti in a soft voice, "Several terrorists coming up the stairs."

"Take care of them," Lao responded.

She, too, had heard the Atchisson and her heart had leapt. Able Team had created such a mighty distraction that the terrorists had forgotten her at the window. She was able to get closer and see what was happening.

The two crews with grenade launchers were at the extreme end of the range for her M-16, so she was relieved when she saw someone else cutting them down. When Able Team started to charge the terrorists remaining around the truck, Lao decided it was time to join the party.

Behind her, the senator triggered his automatic weapon. There was a loud scream and the pounding feet retreated downstairs. Then Lao heard no more as she leaned out the window and emptied her weapon into the defending forces below. They had forgotten her and now was the time to send reminders.

The main body of troops split at the gate. Most entered the grounds with about thirty-odd running toward the tree to take out the sniper. Bolan drove the car off the road and went EVA. He double-timed along the backtrack of the Cuban elimination force. The tree stood in an undeveloped lot and the shrubbery was dense. The Cubans had surrounded the sniper before Bolan had them in sight.

Suddenly another weapon opened up. Bolan heard the steady crack of a rifle. Someone in another tree fifty yards away was picking off the

Cubans under the first tree. Immediately ten faded into the bush to close in on the second sniper. Another few raised their assault rifles to rake the branches above them.

Bolan's MP-5K spoke first, spraying the area with withering fire. Rifles dropped, men screamed, those who survived buried their faces in the ground.

Bolan dived to the ground when a burst of gunfire split the leaves where he had been standing. He kept rolling until he hit the base of another large tree; he lay still long enough to replace the empty clip in the subgun.

He poked his head around the trunk and a hail of bullets drove him back. He pulled a defensive grenade from a blacksuit pouch and tossed it toward the base of the sniper's position. He followed the blast around the tree, using short bursts from the MP-5K to finish off those few who had not succumbed to the grenade. But he was too late to help the second ambusher.

The Cubans had surrounded the second tree and five had emptied their weapons into it. A short dark man fell to earth. From the branches above Bolan, a rifle opened up with single shots, wasting the terrorists who had killed the dark man.

Bolan called up to the sniper. "Coast is clear. You can come down."

STEW WILLIAMS kept squeezing the trigger until his finger became numb. He had seen his partner fall under the Cubans' guns.

He came back to his senses only when he had emptied his second 20-round clip. Then he heard the voice below him. He shifted and peered over the edge of the crude platform.

It was the man he had been ordered to kill! At his feet were the bodies of the terrorists who had been about to kill Williams.

The man called him to come down. Williams shouldered his weapon, put extra clips in his pocket and began the laborious descent from the tree, covered and protected by the man he had been sent to execute.

Bolan spared only a quick glance to see that the sniper was coming down from his post. He spent the rest of the time watching for any stragglers who might ambush them. But there was no one around.

Mack Bolan and Stew Williams stood at the base of the laurel oak, their eyes locked on even height.

"You weren't up there waiting to help Able Team," Bolan said. It was a statement, not a question.

"No. Our orders were to wait and hit you. To allow the Cubans to take care of the other force."

"And now?" Bolan asked.

"Now I do what my conscience says."

Bolan asked no more questions. He merely nodded. "Let's see if we can help some more."

The two warriors took off through the vacant lot to engage the Cubans who were defending the supply trucks.

Bolan and Williams burst through the hedge in time to see enemy troops retreating into the house. Bodies littered the area; Able Team was running quickly from the direction of the garden, followed by Wendy Pitt. Bullets flew from the main party of terrorists, who were working toward the house from the road.

Politician was the first member of Able Team to spot Bolan. With a yell of anguish he knocked Wendy Pitt to the ground and threw his body on top of her. The big M-203 tracked toward Bolan.

Lyons took in the situation with a glance. He didn't bother to ask questions; he accepted facts. Bolan was there—how, he had no idea. Bolan was a threat to their charge, but he must be used. The battle odds were too long as it was. Lyons stepped into Politician's line of fire.

"An Oriental girl. In the house. One of ours. Will you get her?" Lyons snapped at Bolan.

Bolan's answer was to break into a run toward the side entrance, following the retreating Cubans. His peripheral vision told him that Able Team was positioning to defend the house and trucks and that the blond sniper was following him into the house.

Upstairs Lao emptied her clip on the terrorists around the truck. She watched as they broke and ran for the house. She knew there was no way to hold the second floor. There were two sets of stairs and she and Pitt could cover only the wide front staircase. And they could only hold out as long as the ammunition lasted.

She ran across the floor and threw herself beside the senator, the big Ruger in her hand. A terrorist's head popped up above floor level on the main stairs. Lao squeezed the trigger. It barked once as she fought to control the rise of the barrel. The head disappeared in a spray of red.

A burst of fire came sweeping down the length of the corridor. It was at too oblique an angle to penetrate the room wall but it snatched the M-16 from Pitt's hands and swept it down the hall.

He jerked back as a hand appeared over the railing of the main stairs, releasing a small, dark object into the room. Lao placed a bullet in the arm, smashing it back out of sight. But it was too late.

Lao saw the grenade bounce into the room. Pitt pushed himself to his knees and dived on top of it. The grenade exploded, scattering parts of the senator all over the room.

Lao's ringing ears told her what had happened, but she had no time to look over her shoulder. Others were trying to poke guns over the main stairwell and a stream of bullets past the doorway announced more Cubans moving down the hall.

Downstairs Bolan followed the terrorists into the house. He waited until they were bunched up in the narrow confines of the back hallway, then triggered a burst from the SMG.

Enemy troops were slammed against the wall and against one another. Bolan emptied the entire magazine in short bursts, transforming the kitchen into a charnel house.

Bolan stepped over the bodies to the stairwell.

Behind him, Williams paused to exchange his weapon for an M-16 dropped by a dead terrorist.

The Executioner slammed home a new clip as he prepared to face the gunners on the stairs ahead.

Bolan cut down three terrorists running toward the room where Lao was trapped. His battle experience gave the Executioner an immediate assessment of the situation on the front staircase.

He pulled a grenade from a pouch, yanked the pin, then lobbed it over the railing into the stairwell. Arms, legs and torsos flew into sight and dropped back down.

"Friend," Bolan yelled as he ran to the stairwell. "Don't shoot, Lao."

Bolan looked over the broken railing around the stairwell. Nothing moved. Then he turned to look inside the doorway of the room.

He spared little attention for the gore splattered around the room. Then a small Oriental woman stepped forward. Her hair was matted with blood and she was calmly thumbing .45 cartridges into a huge revolver.

"The senator?" Bolan inquired, taking in the chunks of flesh scattered around the room.

The woman nodded as she slipped the gun back into the holster slung over her shoulder. The eyes that sized up Bolan and Williams were serene. There was no trace of fear. There was only the throb on her neck of the heart pumping in response to the high adrenaline flow experienced by a trained warrior in action.

When she spoke, her voice was low and controlled, her accent slight and reflecting a good education. "You could only be Mack Bolan. I've no idea how you arrived, but you're certainly a welcome sight."

Bolan couldn't suppress a grin. "So are you."

Bolan strode past her into the room to look out the window and assess the situation.

Able Team was still defending the corner of the house by the trucks, but a large body of men had split off from the main Cuban force and was coming up the far side of the estate to get at Able Team from the back of the house.

Bolan whirled and started to run. He called over his shoulder, "Work to do."

Lao and Williams fell in behind him, arming themselves on the run with extra weapons.

Bolan descended the stairs to the living room, which was at the front of the house. The Cuban troops were coming straight at this portion of the mansion. He smashed out a window, then used the subgun to cut down the first rank of attackers. These were not untrained soldiers, Bolan knew, as he watched the enemy hit the dirt and begin to worm their way toward their objective.

Beside him Bolan heard Lao and the CIA agent knocking out windowpanes to give themselves a field of fire. But the Cubans were already dropping farther away from the house to go around it in a larger circle.

Bolan hurled a chair through a window and dived outside. He would have to trust Lao and Williams to hold off the strays. Williams held his post and continued to pin the enemy, but the fiery little Oriental was on Bolan's heels, keeping up with his long strides.

Bolan and Lao headed for some shrubbery and threw themselves flat. Each peered around one side and opened fire at the Cubans who were surprised by the maneuver and lost four more of their members before going to ground. Bolan and Lao both rolled away from the bushes as bullets sliced through the leaves, seeking flesh.

The two warriors left their refuge and sought better cover. Bolan spotted a slight dip in the terrain and leaped over the lip of an embankment. He and Lao used the lull to reload their weapons.

It was now nearly nine minutes since Bolan had taken a hand in the battle. He knew Able Team must have been fighting for six or seven minutes before that.

The firefight had developed into major battle.

The Executioner peered over the crest of the knoll to assess the situation.

The enemy had taken root in the cabana, which was located between the trucks and the driveway. The thick hedge that screened the cabana from the roadway had given the terrorists a false sense of security.

The big soldier intended to come around the edge of the hedge and make his approach on the terrorists' flank.

Bolan and Lao started to move, keeping the dense cedar foliage between themselves and the cabana, when suddenly a limousine wheeled into the driveway.

Bolan recognized Maceo in the front passenger seat, and swung up the MP-5K toward the car. But there was no time to fire. The driver swerved the big car toward them and trod on the gas. Lao and Bolan dived between the hedge and the cabana.

Lao covered their retreat while Bolan kept alert for any terrorists watching the rear of the small building.

Maceo leaped from the car and pulled his troops to the mouth of the driveway to stop several other cars and to organize the troops who emerged.

Bolan could not see them through the hedge, but from the sounds of it, concluded there were more than twenty men getting ready to charge from the entrance of the driveway.

Bolan and Lao found themselves lying on their stomachs with nothing but a hedge for concealment. On their right was the sheer wall of the wooden cabana, which sheltered another thirty terrorists now exchanging gunfire with Able Team.

The Executioner could hear a hoarse voice issuing commands in Spanish, preparing for a mass attack against Ironman, Politician and Gadgets.

Bolan emptied the rest of his magazine into the base of the hedge that ran along the side of the property. He changed clips, then charged into the hedge, knocking over enough of the cedar shrubs to make an escape exit to the vacant land beside Pitt's estate.

"As soon as they start to charge us, empty your gun and get out through the side hedge," Bolan commanded Lao.

Lao nodded and crept closer to the edge of the hedge, waiting.

Bolan went around the cabana where the terrorists had been watching the backtrack. He found a window and waited. As soon as he heard Lao's weapon open fire, he smashed the MP-5K through the opaque glass and hosed the inside of the cabana. Then, changing clips as he ran, he followed Lao through the hole in the hedge. They threw themselves flat in the long grass and waited. Bolan had only one spare clip left for his subgun.

Bolan's plan worked. Maceo led his hand-picked brigade around the corner of the hedge just in time to meet a countercharge by the terrorists stumbling out of the cabana.

By the time they sorted out that both groups were on the same side, they were another twenty men short. Some were killed by other terrorists, some were chopped down by Able Team bullets. The Stony Man warriors had closed in as soon as they saw the terrorists break from the cabana.

Politician fired continuously, putting out HE grenades as fast as he could load them into his M-203. The grenades caused the massed terrorists to fall to pieces.

Lyons stalked along the fence row toward the gate, his Atchisson booming. Terrorists found themselves in the open against a withering hail of explosives and shotgun fire. The terrorists panicked, broke for the central garden around the swimming pool, leaving their dead and dying behind.

When Bolan saw that Able Team had begun the attack, he led Lao around the edge of the property and back in behind the new arrivals, Maceo and his specialist team.

First Maceo had been shaken by finding that he had been engaged in battle with his own men. Suddenly more fire was added from behind. He and his specialists also broke, running for the garden.

Maceo's proud army of more than a hundred soldiers found itself reduced to twenty blood-soaked wretches, trapped by a fancy pool. Gunfire was coming in relentlessly from all sides. The area was surrounded.

All six avengers moved in on the garden area. Bolan, Lao, Williams and Able Team. Anything that moved was shot.

The Cubans who had arrived with Maceo had only handguns, as they had not had time to be issued M-16s. Many of the guns were empty. The small group panicked and clustered ten feet from the pool. The circle was tightening, forcing them into the open or into the water.

At this point, they looked to their leader for inspiration. But instead, they found a fat little man huddled at their feet, his hands covering his head.

He was whimpering, "Please, help me."

The terrorists were filled with disgust at the sight of Maceo cowering on the ground. The Cuban troops turned and emptied their guns into their commander.

All of them were cut down before they had a chance to turn back toward the enemy. Twenty minutes after the battle had started, the firefight was over.

The lawn and garden lay in shambles. The gunfire near the park had ceased and the sirens were getting closer. The six blood-drenched warriors met at the edge of the circular pool.

"The police. We have to get Mack through their lines," Lyons said.

"The hearse," Gadgets suggested. He broke into a run toward the garages.

Lyons snapped, "Someone collect these damn flowers to fill the hearse."

Politician turned and made his way back to check Wendy Pitt's safety.

Carl Lyons looked across the pool at Mack Bolan.

"Good job, Mack."

Bolan looked around at the carnage and did not say anything.

Williams pulled up the blossoms, heaping them in a pile beside the driveway.

Politician approached, the M-16 still in one hand and the other hand firmly grasping Wendy Pitt's. She clutched the small M-11 in her right fist. When they reached the edge of the pool, Wendy looked up and saw Bolan for the first time—saw the image imprinted on her subconscious. Without hesitation the M-11 came up and her finger held down the trigger.

Bolan was thrown backward, his weapon flying from his grasp.

Before anyone else could react, Pol's huge M-16/M-203 hybrid came up, the tip of its barrel touching her left temple. He pulled the trigger once and she fell face forward into the pool, the blood turning the water pink.

Rosario Blancanales stood staring down at the long yellow hair rippling on the surface of the pool. As he stared the body sank.

Pol stood motionless, remaining silent.

Lao was the first to reach Mack Bolan. A red trickle coursed down over his ear to the left shoulder of his blacksuit.

"Minor damage to his head, but he'll live," she announced. She rolled the body over.

By the time the hearse arrived, the sirens were incredibly close. In a frantic scramble they put Lao and the unconscious form of Mack Bolan into the back of the hearse and heaped on all the flowers that Williams had collected.

Lyons leaned in over the wheel, through the driver's window of the hearse, and locked eyes with young Zansky.

"Get him through the police lines," Lyons growled.

"Yes, sir," he said.

Williams slid into the front seat of the hearse beside him. Fred Jr. checked to make sure the two people were well concealed under the flowers and then began a slow drive away from the battleground.

Gadgets and Ironman stood in the driveway and watched the vehicle disappear just as the first of the police cars came screaming into sight. Neither had anything to say.

Standing at the edge of the pool, Politician continued to stare at the long golden tresses waving from the bottom.

Gadgets walked back to where Blancanales stood and placed an arm around Pol's shoulders.

"Let's go, Pol. You had to do it."

DON PENDLETON'S EXECUTIONER
MACK BOLAN

Sergeant Mercy in Nam...The Executioner in the Mafia Wars...Colonel John Phoenix in the Terrorist Wars...Now Mack Bolan fights his loneliest war! You've never read writing like this before. By fire and maneuver, Bolan will rack up hell in a world shock-tilted by terror. He wages unsanctioned war—everywhere!

GOLD EAGLE

Available wherever paperbacks are sold.

GET THE NEW WAR BOOK AND MACK BOLAN BUMPER STICKER FREE!

Mail this coupon today!